THE FINAL NOTE

BY: MS. CAROL HULSE- MAYWEATHER

DEDICATED TO: I CAROL-HULSE MAYWEATHER, DEDICATE THIS BOOK TO WOMEN EVERYWHERE OF ALL AGES AND FROM ALL WALKS OF LIFE. I PRAY THAT AS YOU READ, YOUR HEART IS UPLIFTED AND INSPIRED TO LOVE AND LIVE THE LIFE THAT GOD SO ABUNDANTLY PROMISES. DESPITE ALL CHALLENGES, CHANGES AND UNFORESEEN CIRCUMSTANCES, THERE IS A LIGHT IN YOU. I ENCOURAGE YOU TO LET IT SHINE.

ISBN-13: 978-1-948605-03-8

ISBN-10: 1-948605-03-1

ACKNOWLEDGEMENTS

We all have something for which to be thankful. Big things, small things, memorable things, and things that we often take for granted. Take a moment and ask yourself: "Where would I be without God's grace and His loving kindness?" I have given much thought to this concept, and that is why I give Him all the honor and praise for my life, the things I have experienced, and for the opportunity to write this book. I also wish to thank the many people who stood by me through this rough and challenging season in my life. I would love to list them individually, but they are too abundant in number. To each of them, I offer a heartfelt, collective thank you for the blessings of their love, compassion, phone calls, prayers, cheer-me-up gifts, social gatherings, books, wisdom, listening ears, and honesty. I dedicate this book to all of you.

This book was a good experience for me, and truly a collaborative effort. Although, I am the author, I must thank ghostwriters Adrienne Patterson, Emily Miller, and Yolanda Allen; and first editor, Lakesha Davis. I must also thank Gina Flythe, who took 42 pages of what was intended to be a final product, and honed it into the journey to which you are about to embark. You are all amazingly talented women, and you were with me every step of the way. Thank You!

To my daughters, Ashley Hulse and Francis Hulse, thank you for loving me and for keeping me busy during this period of adjustment.

To my sisters, words cannot express my gratitude. Shola Walker, you are a model sister; and you were never too busy to listen to me. Whether I was crying or venting, you never wavered.

To my cousin, Gylaunda Henderson, you have always been a loyal cousin. You even took the time to read the manuscript draft. All of you encouraged me, loved on me, and believed in what I wanted to do.

Last, but definitely not least, I humbly thank my mother, Mary Ann Walker, who has never left my side. You are the earthly rock in my life. During my roughest moments, you were the essential breath of air for me when, at times, I thought I would suffocate. I love, admire, and appreciate you, Mom!

ABOUT THE AUTHOR

Carol Daniell Hulse Mayweather resides in Augusta, Georgia. She has been a cosmetologist and personal business owner for more than 25 years. Carol enjoys dancing, cooking, traveling, and family time. She has always taken pride in being the best mother and grandmother possible, and her family means the world to her. Teaching, and most importantly actively listening to her children remains a priority in her life. Carol's honesty, loyalty, and positive attitude make her a magnet for many people. Her friendship is a valuable asset.

It is Carol's hope that the following pages will serve as a valuable teaching tool to all who read this book. She stands victorious and wants readers to know that God delivered her from darkness and restored her happiness, and He can do the same for them. Writing this book has taught her valuable lessons. She has learned about forgiveness, not giving up on her dreams, and the journey to overcoming. It is a fact that we all have a path to take to get to our destiny, and it is not always the easiest or the prettiest process. No matter the situation, if we have faith and stay on the course, we can make it. Moreover, when we do not know exactly what to do or when we have done all that we can do, we must just *BE QUIET, WAIT, BE PATIENT, and BE STILL.*

Carol's faith empowered her to terminate an unfit relationship centered on a less than undeserving spouse. While not knowing what her future would be, she was brave enough to say goodbye, and trust that God would take care of her. New beginnings are often times hidden beneath so much grief. Carol wants her readers to know that faith can definitely reward you with a new outlook on love. As stated in Isaiah 41:10, "Do not fear, for I am with you, do not be dismayed, for I am your God. I will strengthen you and help you. I will uphold you with my righteous right hand;" If you are dealing with a broken heart, hold on, have faith, trust God -- your help is on the way.

Prelude

[A brief introduction or preface before something longer takes place. In music, it is often (but not always) a short passage at the beginning of a longer piece of music.]

I remember the sun shining brightly outside, and its warm rays kissing my face as I entered his car. Lately, I had barely been able to focus due to the recent incidents in our marriage. Here we were driving to a marriage counselor's office after 12 years of marriage. There was no communication between us, and the five-minute drive seemed like it took hours. All I could think about was how the world as I knew it was now upside down. Occasionally, I would glance over at my husband and wonder who this man was. You see, he had always been charming; however, now his scent, the sound of his voice, even the thought of his touch made my skin crawl. In an effort to break the silence, he spoke to me, but I had no words to return. I only gave him a nod to acknowledge that I had heard him. When we arrived, he demonstrated polite and well-mannered behavior as he opened the door for me. His kind gesture forced me to give him a weak smile. However, when he offered his hand to help me up the stairs to the counselor's office, I quickly grabbed the rail.

We entered the office of Dr. R.D. Peak, a well-known marriage counselor. "Hello," he said as he introduced himself when we entered the room. My husband did all the talking. I was coherent and I heard him speaking, but I was completely numb of pain. His indiscretions were weighing heavily on me. I had so many thoughts going on in my head. *How did we get here? Where did our marriage go wrong? Do I know what love really is? Have I ever experienced love? What have I done? Who is the man/monster? How and why did this happen to me?*

Contents

CHAPTER 1 – OVERTURE

[A piece of music that is an introduction to a longer piece, especially an opera. Also, a communication made to someone in order to discuss or establish something.]

It all began 30 years ago; I remember falling in love early in life. The first time I saw Lewin, my high school sweetheart, he was near the school's front office talking with one of the teachers. He was a slender young man with an average build and a nice smile. His haircut stood out to me. He had this high top fade with a part on the side and low cut in all the right places. I knew I had caught his eye and God knows he had caught mine. A few days later, he walked up to me and said, "Hey Carol, I'm Lewin. Where are you headed?" I was shocked that he knew my name, but impressed that he had taken the time to ask around about me. It took every ounce of restraint to keep from exposing every one of my teeth in a big goofy grin. I smiled at him, demurely, and told him I was going to math class. He walked with me there and we talked just those few moments; but I knew that I wanted to talk with him again. We did not have a care in the world. We were just two kids exploring life together. Every morning we would meet at our lockers and walk down the halls hand and hand. Taking walks through the park was our thing. We enjoyed walking and talking about everyday happenings. On our dates, we could only afford McDonald's and Burger King; but we felt like we were dinning on steak and potatoes. Whenever we were apart, I recall us being on the phone together for hours at a time. My mom would constantly remind me of the time until her patience ran thin. At that point, she would just tell me to get off the phone. Many times, I would want to call him right back, but I knew that was risky. Life seemed to be perfect for us at the time. It would all soon change, when I found out that I was pregnant.

One day after school, Lewin and I met up to go to grab a burger. However, my stomach just turned over. The smells made it almost unbearable for me to be in the restaurant, so I just told him I did not want anything. I got up the next morning and took a bite out of an apple to curb my hunger. Apparently, my stomach was against that too, because within minutes that apple came back up along with whatever else I had eaten the day before. The nausea and vomiting went on for a few more days as if I had a virus or something. Then it happened! I missed my period and what was probably making me ill became clear. I did not know what to do. *Is this really happening?* My first thought was to tell Lewin. The next day, we went on our usual walk around the park. I was scared because Lewin was only a year older than I was. Therefore, I did not know what to expect. I had seen and heard of girls in my situation telling their partners that they had gotten pregnant, and the parents would immediately deny the baby or demand that the girl get an abortion. So naturally, I was concerned. I thought back on all our time spent together and how much we loved each other and just hoped for the best. I finally gathered the courage to spring the news, "Lewin, I think I'm pregnant." "What" he yelled shockingly.

"I think, I'm pregnant," I said more confidently this time. "Are you sure," he questioned me further. "No, I am not sure, but I've been sick for the past two weeks and I missed my period. So, I know it's not the flu," I said awaiting his full reaction. He remained calm and told me we needed to be certain before we jumped to conclusions. We decided to go to one of the local hospitals. There we were in the waiting room and they called my name. I was feeling ashamed and as I walked up to the nurse, she gave me this scrutinizing look. I imagined she knew why I was there. Lewin, who had originally planned to wait for me in the lobby, jumped up beside me and asked her, "Which way are we going, Ma'am?" The nurse cut her eyes at him and asked me, "Do you want him to come back with you?" I smiled and said, "Yes, Ma'am," -- happy that he was being so supportive.

At this point, we headed to the back room where the nurse gave me a cup for a urine sample. I did as she instructed and she later came and collected it. Lewin and I sat there silently. I had no idea what he was thinking, but my mind was racing. I was freaking out from within. I thought we had been so careful. *What am I going to do with a child? What are my parents going to say? How am I going to go to church and be an example for God?* Thoughts and heavy worries that I had not considered before took over my mind. The door finally opened -- it was the doctor. "Hi there, how are you two doing today?" she asked more so out of habit than concern. Trying not to prolong the results, we gave a short "Fine" in response. "So what brings you in?" she asked continuing with her standard routine questions. I was thinking to myself, *"Did she not read the chart?"* However, that was my anxiousness speaking. I went on to express to her that I had been sick for the past two weeks and that I had missed my period. The doctor said, "I understand your concern. Nurse Thompson took your urine sample to our lab. She will be back up as soon as the test is completed. In the meantime, I need you to lay back on the table for me." I lay down as she put on her gloves and pulled my shirt up and began to feel around my stomach area. I thought to myself, *"Can she feel it? Is there a person inside me?"* After a few light presses, she pulled my shirt down and told us to follow her to her office. There we were waiting again. We still had no words to say to one another. Lewin finally broke the strain of silence in the room by giving me a hug and a kiss on my forehead. Then the doctor walked in and sat at her desk. She looked me in the eyes and said, "Sweetie, you are pregnant." The rest of what she said was a blur. Lewin and I headed for his car. He looked at me, grabbed my hand and said, "I can't believe that you and I have made something special growing inside of you." Neither of us knew what to expect, but we knew that the next step was to tell our parents.

Weeks had passed since the confirmation of my pregnancy. I felt like I was about to burst. I had to tell someone so I headed to my friend Stephanie's house.

Surprisingly, my friend, Karen was also there. My baby sister, Angel, insisted that she come along with me. I did not have much choice so I carried her with me. When we arrived at Stephanie's house, I told them, "I got some news to tell you girls." Instantly, they were alert and all ears as I attempted to whisper, because Angel was within an earshot, "I'm pregnant." It was finally out. They asked the typical questions: what was I going to do, did my parents know, and did Lewin know. We talked for a good while, but I had no direct answers for the questions they had asked. I knew Angel heard everything, so before we left, I looked at her and said, "You better not tell anyone." Angel was loyal and she honored my request and kept my secret. Meanwhile, my morning sickness was getting worse. Being at school with all the different scents did not help one bit.

Keeping my pregnancy secret from my parents began to weigh heavily on my conscious. I knew they would be angry and disappointed in me. There were times when I thought I was ready to tell them, but my nerves got the best of me. So I decided against it. Shortly afterwards, God sent me a message through the pastor. My family loaded up to go to church one Sunday. The message that day was on God's love for his children and forgiveness. Then something touched me and gave me the assurance that it was the right time. At some point after dinner, my mom and I just so happened to be the only ones in our kitchen. I said, "Mama, I have something to tell you." She stopped what she doing and looked at me. With tears in my eyes and not knowing what to expect I said, "I'm pregnant." She went back to cleaning, but her face revealed her disappointment. Of course, abortion was out of the question because I knew my family did not believe in it. My mom's silence was comforting because she did not make me feel ashamed, abandoned, or unloved. As mom accepted my pregnancy, she did little things to let me know everything would be all right. In fact, our relationship grew stronger as time passed. Months flew by, and finally at the age of 16, on September 20, 1988, I gave birth to my beautiful daughter, Ashley.

Life was certainly different now. Honestly speaking, if it were not for my mother, I would not have known what to do with my new daughter. I quickly realized that there were no books or detailed descriptions of what to do with a child. Therefore, I was in the OJT (on-the-job training) of being a mother -- this included the late night feedings, changing diapers, cleaning her, and looking after her well-being. Likewise, Lewin would come by to help and provide what he could.

After about a year of juggling a newborn baby, school, and a job, I began thinking about making some changes. Sometimes when you put yourself in adult situations you have to make adult decisions. The decision that I made is one that I regret to this day. I decided to drop out of high school just before my senior year. I was under my parent's roof with my daughter, and they had to provide for my younger school-age sister. Looking at my mom and dad's example, I knew what was important to me. Therefore, it was necessary that I be able to provide for my own child as my parents did for our family and me. I did not want Ashley to suffer, so, I left school and turned my part-time job at a local fast food restaurant into full-time employment. At this time, Lewin worked two jobs and even though I was working full-time, I still needed assistance. Due to my low income, I received full assistance benefits. Despite this, Lewin and I decided to move into our own place.

CHAPTER 2 – HARMONY

[Several notes played together to form chords (three or more musical notes played at the same time) in some type of progression, is known as a harmony. In general, harmonies form a pleasing sound.]

Ashley, Lewin, and I first moved into a little one-bedroom apartment. We bought Ashley a bassinet and placed it at our bedside. We then got a couch and a television for the living room. It was not easy at all, but we made it work -- our little family. Lewin and I were two young people in love. We considered marriage, but we did not feel it was a priority or a necessity at that time. One day, my mom told me that one of their rental properties had become vacant and asked if we would like to rent it. We moved out of that apartment so fast that I do not remember even locking the door behind us. My family's rental was a small two-bedroom house with a full kitchen, living room, dining area, and a sitting room. It was a definite upgrade from the apartment, and we finally had a place to call home. We continued to work as usual; and whenever I had a little free time, I would try out different hairstyles on myself. Likewise, friends and family members would often ask me to do their hair, as well. Hairstyling became an outlet for me. Life seemed to be coming together slowly, but surely. One day, we started talking and decided that we had everything we needed, so why not make it official? Therefore, we jumped into Lewin's Nissan Sentra, and headed to South Carolina.

It was winter, but the weather was fair -- just cool enough with little sharp gusts of wind here and there. As we walked up the steps of the Aiken County courthouse, the wind whipped once and brought a tear to my eye. Lewin saw it, smiled and wiped it away from my cheek. In hindsight, the wind did not cause me to tear up; the tear came when I visualized this new chapter of my life with my first love. In my heart, even my spirit, I knew that at that moment I was on the right path. On the first day of February 1990, Lewin and I were married in a private ceremony. We had stepped into that courtroom as just Lewin and Carol; but we came out as husband and wife. Because of our secret nuptials, there was no reception awaiting us. Accordingly, we stopped for dinner just off the highway on the way home. It was a little southern-style place, nothing to write home about. We bowed our heads together and gave thanks for our food as the server placed our plates down in front of us; but I said a different prayer of thanks. I thanked God for getting us through this last year, for Ashley, for my husband, and for the family and friends who had stuck by us. At that moment, it struck me that we would have to tell our families that we had gotten married without them; and we needed to tell them right away.

Right away turned out to be the following day, when we went to my parents' house to pick up Ashley. I wondered if they would be disappointed that we did not think to include them. When we walked in the house, my parents were watching television, and Angel was playing with Ashley on the floor. After I got everyone's attention, I shared the news that we had just gotten married. My family was happy and they congratulated us. My worries instantly dissipated -- everything turned out just right.

It was just the three of us, but soon it would be four. Yes, I was pregnant with our second child. We had not planned to expand our family so soon, but we knew we could manage. With the support of our family and our faith in God, we believed that we would be fine. My pregnancy was progressing well, but we did not have a phone in the house. Understandably, my husband did not want his pregnant wife at home alone with a toddler and no transportation, especially in case of an emergency. As a result, he began taking me to my mom's home before he went to his evening job. In addition to his two jobs, Lewin also joined the local National Guard unit. He was required to report every month for weekend training. Although we did not get to spend as much time together as a family, we had everything we needed. Ashley was getting bigger by the day and we wanted to capture every moment of her youth. For that reason, we had cameras flashing all the time. I would sometimes imagine my family in our first picture together. Of course, we would distribute our holiday photos to all our family and friends. Yes, I often told myself, everything would be fine.

One thing about life that I know about life is that just when you think you have a little grip on it, life will change becoming like granules of sand slipping through your clasped fist. In other words, no matter how tight you hold on, it is bound to slip out. Lewin had received notice that he would deploy immediately for a tour in the Gulf War. That announcement was hard-hitting, I was terrified, and I did not know what I was going to do. I was not even sure if the baby would arrive before he left. The news loomed over my head like a dark cloud. I knew we should not expect the worse, but it was a heavy burden. After all, it was a WAR. One day, I felt a powerful urge to pray for my husband. I fervently asked God to keep my husband safe -- especially if he ended up in the line of fire. Weeks had passed since we learned about the deployment, and Lewin could see the concern I felt inside. We talked about it and while he was comforting me, he assured me that he wanted to make it back home safely to us. In addition, my due date was just a few weeks away and we were getting things ready for the baby's arrival.

CHAPTER 3 – ELEGY, LAMENTO & LACRIMOSO

[Elegy: A piece of music that expresses grief or sorrow. Lamento: Mournful and sad. Lacrimoso: Tearful and mournful.]

I will never forget the date. It was December 14, and I was nearly nine months along in my pregnancy. Lewin had to work his part-time job that night. As normal, he dropped Ashley and I off at my parent's house. He let us out of the car, gave our baby a big hug and said "Daddy loves you." He then stood up, gave me a kiss and told me he loved me, too. As Ashley and I walked towards the house, I turned around to find that Lewin was still there waving to me standing outside his beloved Nissan. That seemed a bit peculiar to me, but in an endearing way. Even though he always waited for us to get into the house safely, the watching us and waving of his hand, almost subconsciously symbolized a bigger goodbye. I took one last look at him pulling away as I stepped into the house, and for some reason, I watched a little longer as he pulled away and continued to drive on down the road. Once inside, I got me and Ashley settled, and did the normal things I did to pass time until Lewin's return.

The night passed quickly. I had planned to watch the news, but I fell asleep at some point. The ringing doorbell awakened me around 11:30 that night. *"Lewin's here to pick us up,"* I thought to myself. However, when I answered the door, it was my father-in-law, not Lewin, standing there. Surprised to see him, I barely got the hello out when he told me that there had been a car accident and that Lewin was dead. The second the words left his lips, my knees, legs, and feet became lifeless all at once. My blouse was wet and heavy as a sudden, uncontrollable rushing river of tears found their escape. My mind instantly started reasoning, *"It can't be true." "Someone, please say it is not true." "Someone made a terrible mistake." "It is not Lewin." "It can't be Lewin." "We have future plans." "We have a family." "We have a new baby coming." "There has been some sort of mix up." "This is CRAZY!"* I do not remember if I actually verbalized those thoughts or if I was even able to say anything at all. I just know that I could hear a voice in my head, my voice, saying those words quickly and repeatedly, as if I was reciting some type of spiritual chanting exercise.

If the sudden, tragic death of a loved one is not enough to deal with, handling the business-type matters associated with death is just as heavy. The very first thing to do was identify

Lewin's body at the morgue. I was not stable enough, physically or emotionally, to go to the coroner's office to identify his body; therefore, our parents decided it was best that my father-in-law do the initial viewing. I was in denial. I was devastated. I was inconsolable. How could this be? Am I really a widow at just 20 years old? Although this may have been true, I replayed that day and those last moments repeatedly in my head. Lewin waving goodbye to us and his Nissan pulling off was the picture stuck on pause in my brain. When I saw the pictures of the accident, it was horrific to see where the truck plowed into my husband's car. In an instant, it was all gone – the man I loved, the car he loved, the life we loved, the husband, the father, the son -- all gone. My daughter lost her father and my unborn child would never know her dad. *"No, this is a nightmare it cannot be real!"* was all I could wishfully think.

My nightmare became a reality the day of the wake. Up until that point, I had not acknowledged that Lewin was actually gone. The funeral home staff asked if everything was okay, and I responded, "Yes." I then asked that I be given time alone with my husband. As I looked at him lying there, I let out a wailing cry. I leaned in to embrace him for the last time. I would have given anything for his body to feel warm again, to feel his arms embrace me, and to hear him just say my name. No matter how much I wanted that, it was not to be. The beautiful man that I knew and loved was gone. His spirit had ascended and the corpse that I was looking at could not respond to me. After spending my desired time alone with *"him"*, I allowed our family and friends in the room to view his body.

When the time came for Lewin's burial, I was still in denial. Family and friends filled the church. Many people attended, but all the faces were just blurs. I looked to my side and saw my daughter resting in my baby sister's arms. The Pastor and others spoke, vocalists sang songs, and others read poems. Nevertheless, I was deaf to it all. Through my tears, I affixed my eyes on that wooden box as many questions rushed through my mind. *"How do I go on?"* *"How am I going to raise these two kids without their father?"* When the service ended, it took everything in me to stand and maintain myself, but I did. I continuously asked God, "Why?" I begged and pleaded with Him and even Lewin himself to come back to me. A piece of me left when the pallbearers took my husband to lay him in his final resting place.

Eleven days had passed and the grief was as fresh as the day it happened. Crying had become like breathing to me. I could not wake up without tears. I was not able to do anything without weeping, and I would wail myself to bed (not just at night, but also throughout the day). I had just lost my husband and I did not have the words to express what I was really feeling. I was hurt, confused, depressed, and drowning in a murky pool of despair. It was Christmas, but I saw no reason for celebration. My two-year-old daughter was clueless to the fact that she had just lost her father. In her mind, it was just another day of playing with her toys. As I watched her playing from my bed, I knew I had to get myself together. I would soon be responsible for two little lives. Besides that, Lewin would not want me wallowing in grief like this. I tried to suppress my grief, but I less than successful. New Year's was here in a blink of an eye. Instead of going out or attending church, I stayed home and looked through the pictures of Lewin and me, and our daughter.

Chapter 4 – Modulation

[The process of changing from one key to another within a musical composition.]

On the 5th day of January, my water broke and I rushed to the hospital. Shortly thereafter, I gave birth to another beautiful baby girl. As happy as any mother is in childbirth, my happiness was tempered with the knowledge that Lewin was not there to see our daughter's birth…he would never hear her first words, see her take her first steps, or hold her in his arms -- not even once. His moments with our oldest daughter, now frozen in time, were limited to a few pictures and the desperate hope that she would somehow remember her father.

Though they never met and could never meet in this life, I wanted to ensure that our youngest daughter knew that her father was a part of her, and how happy he was that we created her. I named her, Francis, giving her his middle name. I tried my best to let my happiness about my beautiful little baby snuff out the sadness I felt over Lewin's death. I did the normal/expected things -- smiling when family and friends visited, cooing and fussing over my little baby girl, and I ordering the traditional pictures taken of Francis at the hospital; but truthfully, depression had already overtaken me. The vision I had of the perfect and complete family shattered into a million pieces when Lewin died. My sadness and grief would have to be afterthoughts because now, I was solely responsible for everything – from taking care of our girls, taking care of our home, taking care of our bills -- just everything. I began to worry about our basic needs. My grief took a back seat to my basic survival instincts. I had two beautiful girls who needed me. Taking care of them was also a way of honoring the memory of their father. I had to get myself out of that deep dark hole, and the only person who could help me was my Father in Heaven. So I fervently prayed for strength, direction and comfort.

Medical professionals say that grief has five stages – denial, anger, bargaining, depression, and acceptance. I am uncertain if the stages happen in a specific order, but I think at this point, I had become angry. I was very emotional and I am unclear as to   whether I was seeking justice or if I needed accountability; but what I did know was that Lewin died because of someone's negligence. Lewin's accident was the fault of a driver in a corporate truck. In fact, the driver had been drinking when he plowed into my husband's car. One would think that even insurance companies had boundaries and would do at least the minimum to correct a wrong. However, they did not. The insurance company gave me the runaround, started talking about red flags, questioning my rights to my husband's estate, and the legality of our marriage. All of this made me even angrier, and gave me a place to focus all of the rage I felt for how my happy life had turned to tragedy. It became evident the insurance company intended to try to take advantage of me -- the young widowed high-school dropout. Well, that is what they thought. God blessed me with an attorney, and we decided to go through with litigation. My attorney was knowledgeable, understanding and dedicated to advocate on my behalf and that of my children and their futures.

I was a little nervous as I headed to the courthouse that day. This was something I had never experienced before and I knew that I was going up against a powerful insurance company. As I approached the doors of the courthouse, the wind whipped around me in gusts, that blew at my dress and disheveled my freshly styled hair. As I pulled open the courthouse door, a mild gust of wind lightly brushed my cheek -- almost like a reassuring touch that gave me a sense of peace. I prepared myself to state the simple but brutal truth of the situation -- their driver was under the influence while operating their corporate vehicle when he killed my husband and left my girls without a father. When the court clerk called my case, we, the plaintiffs, gave our statement and presented the reports and evidence that we had gathered. The defendants gave their statement and attempted to downplay me, as well as the facts of the case. It did not take much time for the judge to make his decision. He ordered the insurance company to pay a settlement to me. This did not bring my husband back, but it did put me on better footing to take care of our daughters and me. Thank you Father God.

I had been staying with my parents since Lewin passed. I could not bring myself to stay at our place – there were just too many memories, things would never be the same, and it would never feel like home to me again. I began my search for a new home for me and the girls. As God would have it, the perfect house for us was the house right next door to my family's home — and it was up for sale. Just like that, my search had ended; and Ashley, Francis, and I moved into our new home in March. With my financial concerns resolved for the time being and my fight for justice concluded, memories of Lewin filled my thoughts and heart. Though I understood that he could not be with us physically, I still needed to feel his presence, and it was important to me that Ashley remembered her daddy and that Francis know who he was. I picked out about a dozen pictures of him, had them blown up, and placed them all around the house. In my quiet time, I would reminisce about my time with Lewin and ponder about how to build a happy life for all of us without him. I knew that I was drifting deeper into depression. I felt it happening, I did not want it to happen, but it had a hold of me and I felt powerless to stop it. Again, I prayed fervently to God Almighty to hold on to me and to place His angels around me, and my children. I had faith in Him, but my faith and resolve were weakening.

CHAPTER 5 – RHAPSODY

[A free-style instrumental piece characterized by dramatic changes in mood.]

One Sunday afternoon, the girls and I went to my parent's house for dinner. I offered to wash dishes after dinner, and found myself gazing absently out the window over the kitchen sink. A beautiful red cardinal flew up and perched on the other side of the window. I had seen pictures of cardinals before, but I had never seen a live one. I watched the cardinal flitter from branch to branch just singing and enjoying the beauty of spring – flowers blooming, leaves filling the tree branches, puddles sparkling from an earlier rain shower. That cardinal did not know what tomorrow held. It did not know what it would eat, or when it would eat next. Yet, this little bird was happy, exuberant and living life in the moment. This tiny, vivid, vibrant and carefree creature captured my attention and somehow it gave me a sense of peace and purpose. I began considering what to do next; I needed to do something for myself. I needed to feel simple joy and to be happy in the moment.

The next morning, I called my mom and asked if she would look after the girls for a while, and she agreed. I had nowhere to go really, but I needed some time and space to think and just get some fresh air. I drove in no particular direction for the first 20 minutes or so, but strangely, I ended up at the park where Lewin and I had our first date. I took in a deep breath of the morning air and just let the rays of sun caress my face. It seemed that the path that Lewin and I used to take was calling out to me. Without a second thought, I went in that direction. I had walked that same path a hundred times over; but this time, I was walking it alone. I wanted to cry, but the tears would not come. Instead, I started taking in the scenery -- the swings (I swung while he pushed); the slide where we shared our first kiss, the tree that I leaned up against when he first told me he loved me, and the bench we sat on after learning that Ashley was growing inside me. Realization set in at that moment that this was a place where I never had to feel sad. In this place, I could relive all the good experiences I had shared here with Lewin. I felt a spirit of blessed serenity come over me. I knew then that I did not need to be afraid of life without Lewin. I did not have to be afraid of anything. Even more so, I knew that Lewin was in God's hands and that God was watching over Ashley, Francis, and me. I believe it was in God's plan that I drove to this place so that I could see that Lewin's memory would never fade from my mind. As long as I had the park, the pictures around the house, and his legacy left through our girls; Lewin would always be there for us, in spirit.

A few of my friends were going out to dinner one night and asked me to join. I had not been out socially in over a year since my pregnancy with Francis. It was weird getting dressed and applying makeup for the first time as an adult. I looked in the mirror and there I was. I was no longer the 16-year-old girl, but the 20-year-old woman and a mother of two. Where would life take me now? I had no idea. We met up at a restaurant in downtown Augusta, caught up on all the happenings in everybody's lives and families. I recall them all greeting me with so much love and care, and during the evening, we often talked about my girls; however, at not one time did any of them mention my late husband. By the end of the night, I had started to feel a little hurt and wondered if they cared. As I mused over it a bit longer, thank goodness that I realized that they wanted to protect my feelings and just have a good time. I love them for that day. They made me feel like a normal 20-year old out for a night on the town with her girls. From that night on, life changed for me.

Chapter 6 – Più mosso and Allegro

[Più mosso: More movement, more motion. A directive to perform the indicated music passage of a composition with more motion or faster. Allegro: Quick tempo, cheerful.]

We finally were starting to spend more time outside the house. The girls and I would make frequent trips to the park even though they did not know that this was a favorite spot for their dad and me. Ashley was a toddler and Francis just several months old, and they enjoyed the park as much as Lewin and I did when we were together. As I pushed Ashley in the swing and watched her go down the slide, I reminisced on the beautiful memories that Lewin and I shared in this space. It gave me the greatest feeling to enjoy those moments with the girls. In a way, it was as if the four of us were all together as I had once pictured it.

I soon started dabbling in hair styling again. At first, it was only for a few close friends and relatives; and of course my own. My sister, Angel, was one of my first regular clients. Although I had no formal training, hair styling was something that I loved doing, I was naturally good at it, and it kept my mind occupied. One day, I received a call from my friend, Stephanie, a junior at Fort Valley State University, inviting me to a fraternity party on that Saturday. At first, I thought that I would feel out of place (since I was not enrolled in college, and I was already a mother of two); but soon curiosity about the college experience tapped me on the shoulder and encouraged me to go. I revisited thoughts of a dinner I had with my friends. They had all spoken of their college escapades and work lives, while I had talked about single-handedly managing a family. Listening to their banter pointedly drilled home the fact that I had missed attending proms, high school graduation, enrolling in college, and just being a carefree single person. Even though I had chosen a different path in life, I still wanted to experience some of that -- even if only temporarily. I quickly told Stephanie that I would come. I left my daughters with my mom, packed an overnight bag, and drove the two and a half hours southwest to Fort Valley, Georgia. It felt almost surreal to me as I walked onto the college campus that Saturday. There were people my age everywhere. Likewise, a few sororities and fraternities were on the lawn stepping and chanting with onlookers cheering. Others were standing off to the side listening to a young man speak about police brutality. He was attempting to rally them to staging a campus protest. Under the shade of the large age-old trees, I assumed that the clusters of people were holding study groups, since they were all holding books and conversing back and forth. Finally, I had found my way to Stephanie's dormitory. When I got to her room, I found her consumed in her books. She was working on a paper that was due the following week. She had to first write it up in draft form, and then go to the library to type it. Anxious to spend time with me, Stephanie wrapped up her work for the day. She took me on a short campus tour of all the basic stops to include the library, student dining, and a few other need-to-know spots that were a part of her daily routine. Before I knew it, daylight was slowly slipping away. We went back up to her room to change for the party. Shortly after, we met up with another friend of Stephanie's in the dormitory lobby, and the three of us headed to the party. Walking into a boom of music, lyrics rang out "let the music take control ... let the rhythm move you" and people were dancing everywhere. If they were not dancing, they were socializing, having a good time playing cards, and eating. I noticed that some of the young men were whispering into young women's ears, some of the women were giggling and entertaining themselves, and some people were just having fun joking around. The night went on without a problem. I warmed up to the party and after refusing about seven requests to dance, I finally offered my hand to someone. To be honest, I probably accepted his request because I liked his high-top fade haircut. After that, I danced all night with Mr. High-Top Fade, Stephanie, and her friend. I do not think I had ever danced so much in my life. When I think about my life up to that point, I KNOW that this was the first time I had ever been out dancing this way.

Around 10 o'clock the next morning, a mere four hours from the time we got in; I decided to head back home. As I drove, I could not stop thinking about how much fun I had over the weekend. I made the decision, at that moment, that it would not be my last time visiting Stephanie; and it surely would not be my last time getting out. That visit also made me eager to visit my friend, Karen, at nearby Georgia Southern University. When I visited Karen, we also did a lot of fun things that college students loved to do.

With my 21st birthday just around the corner in November, I decided to make my celebration big. I planned a grand party for myself and added new and old friends to my invitation list. This party would be the perfect way to sustain the lightheartedness that I was feeling. I felt young and vibrant again, and I wanted my party to be lively like the ones I attended while visiting my friends at college. I wanted great music, good food, and festive decorations – the works. I wanted everything to be perfect. This party would be like a coming out for me. Coming out of sadness, coming out of mourning, coming out into a world of possibilities. The party was a tremendous success. I looked great, I felt great, and everything went as planned. I felt as if I was starting a new chapter in the book of my life, and that my life and disposition were on an upswing.

CHAPTER 7 – MENO MOSSO AND ALLEGRETTO

[Meno mosso: Less movement, less motion. Allegretto: Not as fast as allegro.]

The weeks following my birthday party were good, and I enjoyed the Thanksgiving dinner and weekend with my family. The year would end soon, and I started to focus on planning Christmas for the girls. It would be an exciting time for them – especially Ashley. The television channels were flooded with toy commercials and she had started to point and ask for certain dolls and toys. Francis was not old enough to ask for anything, but whenever a toy commercial appeared on the television screen, she would stare like a deer in headlights. She would bounce up and down and the smile on her plump little face would warm my heart. This was going to be a great Christmas. I was going to get a big Christmas tree, decorate it with brightly colored ornaments, and fill every empty space below it with gifts for the girls. Yes, it was going to be a great Christmas.

On December 13, my mother called and asked if she could keep the girls for a few days. I thought this was a great idea. It would give me an opportunity to do some deep cleaning without them underfoot. She picked them up just before dinner and I quickly addressed the list of tasks that I needed to complete. I checked several things off my list, and I went to bed feeling a sense of accomplishment. I woke up the next morning with a heavy heart. I could not focus and breathing was difficult. I got out of bed, went to the bathroom, and started splashing my face with cold water. As I walked back to the bedroom, and passed a wall calendar and realized that it was the anniversary of Lewin's death. I must have dreamed about that fateful day because I woke up with my body reacting physically and emotionally. At that point, it dawned on me that my mom remembered the anniversary, and had thoughtfully come by the night before and offered to take the girls for a few days. My mother's thoughtfulness allowed me time alone to deal with what had happened to my family on December 14, 1990. Although my body ached as if I had the flu, there was nothing wrong with me medically. I succumbed to the feelings and just lay in bed holding myself in an attempt to comfort the girl inside me who had lost her husband a year ago. Throughout that experience, I kept remembering my visit to the park and the confidence that Lewin's spirit and memory would always be with me. However, in spite of that, my emotions overtook me. I tried to get up and get myself dressed, but soon found myself in my closet wailing. All the partying, all of the hanging out, and everything I had done to feel whole again seemed to be in vain. Regardless of what I tried to portray or be on the outside, the young grieving widow had reappeared and she wanted and needed her husband. *What could I do to make her go away? How could I get out from under this cloud?* I thought of going to my parents' to get the girls, but I realized that would only make things worse. In order to get the girls, I would have to enter through the same door where Lewin's father had delivered the devastating news a year ago. Instead, I did the only thing that felt rational to me in that moment. I went to the park to be with Lewin.

The changes in the weather kept me from visiting the park for months. We had had so much rain that going anywhere outside was a gamble. It was a bit cloudy outside, but I needed to be there. First, I sat in one of the swings and just let the wind gently sweep across my face. I surveyed the park from my swing and saw all of our favorite spots. I felt as if I was living a never-ending nightmare, and I wondered if it would be like this every year on the anniversary. Leaning back in the swing and thrusting my lower limbs forward and backwards caused the swing to begin to gain height. In fact, it felt as though Lewin was pushing me in the swing. Each time I drew my legs back, it seemed like a force from behind me pushed me higher. As I continued swinging, I felt wonderful, radiant warmth deep inside. It was beautiful, it was exuberant, and it bubbled up from within as laughter. With each sway forward, I found that I could not hold back the laughter -- it came bursting out. I stayed on that swing laughing until the rain started falling, and day had turned to night. Even then, I did not leave. I got off the swing and just walked around and around the park, as if in a trance. *Slush, slush, slush*, I could hear my shoes sloshing from the rainwater. My clothes dripped from the aftermath of the downpour; yet, I could not have cared less. I needed to be there at that particular moment. The rain was like a symbolic cleansing from heaven.

I was not worried about getting wet. I was not worried about the fact that I was alone in the park at night. I trusted that a force bigger than myself had led me to the park. I had faith that that same force was protecting me. I believed that I could slowly walk through my emotions, through my fears, through my emptiness; and with each drip from my clothing and slush of my shoes, the heaviness was coming off me. I was so deeply engrossed on my metamorphosis that I did not notice when the rain stopped.

CHAPTER 8 – GIOCOSO

[Music played in a cheerful or playful way.]

I t was time to celebrate Francis' first birthday. With family and a few close friends, I threw her a small party at Chuck E. Cheese. There were balloons, cake, ice cream, hot dogs, hamburgers, and of course, pizza. It was a happy occasion, yet there were no cameras. For someone who had once tried to capture every special moment in photographs, I then realized that I had not taken a picture of Francis or Ashley, in my home in over a year. I watched my girls that day with gratitude that God had allowed me to see them grow. Their beautiful innocence and rich laughter gave me life and strength every day. Still, I just did not want to take any pictures. After the party, I took the girls home and bathed them. I dressed them in their Beauty and the Beast nightgowns and put them in bed with me. Their little bodies snuggled close to me and I breathed in the sweet scent of baby lotion and baby powder. As the three of us lay in bed that night, after a beautiful little celebration for my baby girl, it hit home that I did not have the perfect family that I had once pictured. Perhaps, that is why I no longer felt the need to take photographs of us. In my mind and in my plan, there should have been a dad in the picture with us. However, my perfect "picture" was forever changed. Dim were the once vivid colors of my life. What was left of my family was still very beautiful, just different from what I imagined. Somehow, I would have to pick up the paintbrush and fill in the spaces that were empty in my life.

January soon turned to February, February thawed to March, and March bloomed to April. Spring was in the air again and I was back in the wind with my friends -- mostly on weekends when they were free and when I could get a babysitter. Some on the outside looking in may have criticized that I had started to take my responsibilities as a mother too lightly; but that was the least of what I was doing. I was a mom every day, 24 hours per day; seven days a week; and months had passed since I had done anything unrelated to being a mom. I had often heard the term, "24/7", and I was now living the reality of it. Therefore, after making arrangements for the care of my daughters, I made plans to spend spring break weekend with my friends. This would be their last college spring break before graduation, and Myrtle Beach, South Carolina was our destination. It seemed that hundreds of other people had the same destination that week because Myrtle Beach was flooded with tourists and vacationers. Music blasted from every direction on the strip. The roar of motorcycles revving up with riders doing tricks, the horns and booming bass of cars, and the calls and whistles of the people on foot filled the air with excitement. Street vendors lined the sidewalks selling everything from swimwear, knock-off designer items, and various seashells *(taken directly from the local beach and should have been free, but tourists were buying them without question)*. Ignoring all of the vendors, the four of us headed for the water. Stephanie sat her portable boom box down in the sand, and we took our shoes off to meet the surf. Initially, we only allowed ourselves to get ankle deep in the water; all of us declined even the thought of getting our hair wet. We wanted to have fun in the water; but between having fun and looking cute, looking cute was definitely the priority! A couple of the girls grew more adventurous and waded out until they were in waist deep. After only a short time, we drew the attention of three young men enjoying the waves, and they gradually made their way over to us. After splashing around for a little bit longer, we all headed for the sand where the boom box was playing a string of popular R & B hits. Before we knew it, we had our own little party right there on the beach.

We laughed, danced, and exchanged the basic information: names, hometown, zodiac signs, favorite music artists, etc. Our newly found friends were prepared to stay with us as long as we would allow. Their group had been grilling nearby, so, they briefly went back to the area and soon returned with their hands and arms filled with enough food, drinks, and snacks for the seven of us. It was obvious that they had further intentions as they enthusiastically chatted up with all of us. Hours passed by like minutes. Since there were three men and four of us women, I decided to be the odd-man-out – gradually separating myself away from group so that the others could match up if they so decided. Although the men were quite handsome and talked a good game, I was enjoying the experience and did not need any additional baggage to carry home. Instead, I sat down on my beach towel, leaned back on my elbows, waited for the sunset, listened to the back and forth, and reminisced on the days when Lewin used to whisper in my ear. Those were the days when I, like my friends, was that giggling girl without a care in the world. This was peaceful tranquility at its best.

Day slowly gave way to the sunset. I am not sure if anyone else even noticed how the golden glow of the sun turned into a beautiful soft rainbow just before disappearing into the horizon. The colors of the sky and the ocean were mesmerizing. Once it began getting chilly, we headed back to our hotel room; but we planned to come back out for nightlife at the beach. We were all feeling upbeat and lighthearted. In fact, Stephanie still had her boom box playing from the beach party. We entered the room loudly, so much so that if the phone had been ringing; we could not have heard it. This was just a brief period to regroup, as we quickly decided that we wanted to change clothes for the night party. Collectively, we decided that we would dress alike in cut-up jeans and tops. We were booked in a double-bed suite with a kitchenette; still there was only one bathroom. As a result, the four of us took turns showering. This caused us to adjust our plans for the night because four separate showers would take a while. We allotted each person 15 minutes in the bathroom – five minutes for the shower, and ten minutes with the lighted mirror. After that, each person would finish dressing in the main bedroom area. Karen hit the shower first while the rest of us passed the time sitting on the couch and sharing a big bag of chips. Stephanie began telling jokes about our high school days. Some of the stories she told were good memories, and some things she revealed for the first time. Some of the other girls could not believe some of the things we had done back in high school. We laughed until our eyes filled with tears and our stomachs ached. After an hour, everyone was ready, and we returned to the beach and partied all night. We continued this same practice almost every day of spring break, with the only changes being what we wore and where we ate. Before we all knew it, the week was over.

It was Sunday morning and the time had come for us all to return to our normal routines. After our sequenced showers and bathroom times, we packed our bags being careful not to pack any of sand that despite our best efforts, was everywhere in the room. After checking out of the hotel, we all headed to a local restaurant for a quick breakfast. We all had so much fun, and we hated that our vacation time together had to end. Each of us played a part in stalling to make the breakfast last much longer than necessary, but we soon had to get up and get on our ways. Outside the restaurant, we hugged each other, said goodbye, and headed back to our pre-vacation places of origin -- Fort Valley State University, Georgia Southern University, and *Carol's Family Home University*.

Driving back home alone in my car gave me time to think about all of my blessings. I thought about how my friends still included me and, even though I was not in college or pursuing similar interests. I thought about all of the little things that my mom did to help me take care of my girls, and what a blessing it was to have her right next door. I thought of how my girls giggled when I bathed them and put them to bed at night. I thought about how they like to look in the mirror after I fixed their ponytails and applied the colorful ribbons and hair bows. I thought about the fact that I had a home – not a dorm room or an apartment, but my own home. That time of reflection during the drive made me appreciate my friends and family just that much more. When I arrived home, I was happy to see my mom and my little girls. I knew that I would immediately return to sole responsibility for everything at *Carol's Family Home University*, but I was still happy to be back. No matter what, my daughters would always be my first priority. I would have to wait to reminisce on those beach parties when my girls were sleeping.

CHAPTER 9 – POCO A POCO AND PRESTO

[Poco a poco: Little by little. Presto: An instruction that a movement or work is fast in tempo.]

Busy with motherhood, it seemed that May came almost overnight. It was time for my friends to graduate from college. Everyone close to me was evolving into another stage of his or her life. Thankfully, my friends and I would talk often, even though some either started summer jobs or began careers in their fields of study. Stephanie phoned me one day to tell me the good news about her new full-time position in Atlanta, Georgia as an account representative. Of course, I was happy for her; but I think I envied her a little too. I wanted something new and exciting for myself. I wanted to feel like my life was also evolving to another stage. I slumped down at the table and ran my fingers through my hair as several questions came to mind. The biggest question was, "What would I do with myself? " My only work experience was when I worked at the fried chicken restaurant. I had certainly outgrown fast-food work and I definitely would not find it financially or emotionally stimulating. My mother owned a drapery shop, but sewing was not my thing either. I lazily continued to play in my hair, as I tried to figure out a career path for myself. After several long strokes through the back of my curled hair, the answer to my question revealed itself. I knew what I was going to do. I was going to build a career doing something for which I already had a knack and a love -- hair styling. I was going to school to study cosmetology.

I gathered and submitted all of the necessary paperwork associated with the application. As soon as I received notification that my application was accepted, I quickly completed the registration process. I was going back to school. I was going to matriculate through a program and earn my certification, just as my friends did with their college programs. Before I knew it, the Monday morning of my first day of cosmetology school came, and I was excited to be pursuing my dream. It felt great to do something in which I would focus solely on myself. I drove to the local beauty college only to discover that I was the first student to arrive. In fact, I was 20 minutes early. Nervously, I entered the building to find a beautiful, tall, and long dark-haired woman with glowing ebony skin. It appeared that she was setting up for the day. Once she realized that I was a student, she gave me a quick look and asked my name. I told her that I was Carol. She continued pulling things from the boxes. The woman quipped, "Well, aren't we the early bird?" Introducing herself as Ms. Young, she pulled a clipboard from one of her packages. "Ugh here you are, Carol, you are the first one here so you can pick your booth. Ms. Young went on to tell me that the room was ready. The instructor was due to arrive shortly after 9 o'clock." In the doorway of the classroom, I paused. I was amazed at how much the room looked just like a real salon. It had stylist booths aligned against the walls with several stations located in the center. Likewise, the walls displayed photos of different hairstyles and product posters. Still stunned in amazement, I made my way around the room to see which station was the perfect fit for me. From the doorway, I walked to the back of the room, then up the center. I stopped at the front center chair. This was the one; I thought to myself. It had a straight view from and to the door. I sat down in what would be my chair for the next nine months, leaned back and took in a deep breath. In that moment of silence, I could not help but think of Lewin. These were not sad thoughts. No, this time I felt that he would be proud of me for pursuing my dream, and trying to do something with my life. This was the beginning of building a career -- a career that would ultimately be the means in which to provide for our girls. I could not help but smile to myself, and think, "Yeah he's proud of me."

Each day, I learned something new in class. I had been styling my own hair for the past couple of years, using my own techniques, and had always received many compliments. Class proved to be quite different. While my novice, self-taught techniques resulted in many popular "hairstyles", I was now gaining an in-depth knowledge of "hair care." I learned about hair and products from a scientific perspective; and I learned the importance of mastering the proper techniques to ensure healthy, positive results. As part of our kit, all students in the class received a mannequin head, professionally known as a "model;" and those models bore the burden of each student's daily learning experiences. Lucky for me, I had another model at home – a live and willing model – my little sister, Angel. The more I learned in class, the more Angel got her hair done. The more advanced my knowledge, the more intricate her hairstyles. Once students mastered the basic techniques and the instructors indicated that the students were ready, the cosmetology school would open its doors to paying customers and allow the students to perform their skills in a salon setting. After a few months of class, I had regular clients coming to the college salon asking specifically for me, and making appointments to be in my chair. My instructor was excited that I already possessed multiple styling skills, and impressed at how quickly I learned the new techniques. She would often question whether I had previously attended another beauty school or had some formal training somewhere else. I would smile politely each time she asked that; but, inside, my spirit would soar. That was the best compliment I could receive from my instructor. Things were going extremely well. I was building friendships with my classmates, and my dream of having a professional career was finally becoming reality. In fact, reality was fast approaching -- whether I was ready for it or not. My classroom and salon training period was soon to be over, which meant that it was time to find work. Therefore, I started to search for a good salon in which I could begin my livelihood. A few of the girls from class were working in the salons they frequented; but that would not be an option for me. Reason being, I styled my own hair and I had not visited a salon for hair care services in about two years.

There was a bulletin board in the school's administration office with job-opportunity postings. One day while I was searching through the listings on the board, Ms. Young happened by and said, "Hello Early Bird, what are you looking for?" I responded that I was searching for a salon in which to work. Ms. Young told me that there were openings at the salon where she received hair care services. She then handed me a card with the owner's information and suggested I give her a call. The next day, I phoned Ms. Sharon Jackson at her salon, and I told her that Ms. Young from the beauty college had referred me. Just like that, she asked when I could get started. I had class through the week and still needed to check with my sitters (Mom and Angel). I told her I could come the following Tuesday. The salon was located in a busy part of downtown. It was hectic and filled with lots of daily traffic. When I started in the salon, my duties mainly consisted of being the "shampoo girl" for Ms. Jackson and one other stylist. Initially, I was excited about my full schedule. After all, I had a part-time job, I was going to school, and I had my girls to care for. I felt like I had not missed a beat, with regard to being responsible member of society. Unfortunately, the every-day interactions, multiple personalities, and even competitive behavior within the salon setting can make one think twice about their chosen profession. I remember an occasion when Clarrissa, one of the third-string employees at the salon, snatched a walk-in client who was to receive services from another stylist. It turned into a big blow. Clarissa and the other stylist were at each other's throats. This dispute over a $30 dollar appointment resulted in harsh words and disrespectful tones toward others; and ultimately, created a negative atmosphere within the salon. Certainly, clients could sometimes be ill mannered or even rude; in fact, I had even heard of clients throwing objects if they did not like the outcome of their hair, or getting involved in heated, inappropriate conversations. However, I did not expect to be working in a setting with an apparent air of hostility each day. I endured this daily trial for as long as I could. I thought about my daughters possibly having to be at this salon with me and witnessing all this drama. I knew that this environment could taint my daughters' understanding of how a young woman should conduct herself. Heck, I was an adult, and this behavior disgusted me. I loved my career, but I just did not love the setting. I knew I had to have my own salon.

CHAPTER 10 – CADENZA AND CRESCENDO

[Cadenza: A solo passage of music, often virtuosic, either written by the composer for improvised by the performer. Crescendo: Gradually louder.]

I began to make plans for my own salon. Initially, I looked at rental spaces in town. They all required substantial work to be converted into a suitable salon space. I found a few spaces that I liked and compared the benefits. I wanted a second opinion so I consulted with my parents. My mom's focus was the location and the equipment that I would need to install. My dad, on the other hand, took a quick review of the building options and said, "Carol, with these rental prices, you could build your own salon." As soon as he uttered those words, the seed found fertile ground in my mind. That afternoon, I hit the ground running looking for local builders to design my salon. I soon learned that the ideal space would require land. The following morning while doing the dishes, my mind was churning with ideas. As with most mornings, I heard the familiar sound of birds chirping and singing happily in my yard. One sound seemed to distinguish itself from the other sounds. Just outside the window, I saw a red cardinal flying around – just flitting from space to space but not going anywhere in particular. Actually, the way it flew upward as if to perch on the empty air struck me as silly. As I continued to look out of the kitchen and into my backyard, I noticed that there was more than enough land for me to build an addition onto my house. I took my idea to my father's friend who owned a construction company; and within the month, they began working on my salon.

In order to open and operate my salon, I had to have my cosmetology license. The only thing standing between my dream and reality was an examination -- I only needed to pass my examination to become a licensed cosmetologist. The cosmetology examination consisted of two parts – a hands-on demonstration, and a written examination. I breezed through the hands-on demonstration, and passed it with *excellence*. I wish I could say the same about the written exam … I failed it. I brushed my failure off and scheduled a retake. After taking the written exam the second time, I waited almost a week for the results. When I saw my score, I pulled out Florida Evans' most famous line from the "Good Times" sitcom, throwing up my hands and screaming, "Damn, damn, damn!" I had failed the exam again. Naturally, doubt set in and I wondered if investing in the construction of the salon addition to my home had been a smart decision. Equally important, I considered all of the time that I had spent studying cosmetology and missing time away from my girls over the last nine months. There was another exam scheduled for the next week, but I decided to set my date for two weeks out to give myself additional study time. During those two weeks, I spent every free moment I had studying the test material and eventually learned it like the back of my hand. When exam date came, I said a prayer, arrived 20 minutes early, chose the best seat for my comfort, and began my test. Finally, my hard work paid off and I passed the exam. By the following week, my new salon addition was complete and I excitedly planned for the grand opening of Carol's Hair Care. My heart filled with pride and jubilance as I decorated my salon and ensured that I had all of the necessary creature comforts for my pending clients. Of course, the best possible item of décor was my framed cosmetology license. Another added blessing was that when I opened my salon doors, several of my beauty school clients walked through them with me.

Within the first 60 days of my opening, word spread quickly and my weekend appointment slots were fully booked as a result. Finally, my business and my family were going great. In fact, I even had time for a social life with my friends; therefore, I had no complaints. At the end of some workdays, I would often sit in my salon and reflect on my journey. Success was no longer a dream, but a reality. Plainly put, I felt tremendously blessed to have success and be a business owner at such an early age.

Aside from my successful business and home life, I was ever mindful of the fact that my daughters were growing older each day. This caused me to begin to think about life down the road and the family unit that I had always pictured. I wondered if there would ever be a man in our lives. I did not spend too much time or energy wondering or worrying about any ifs. Instead, I spent the next two years building my clientele and watching my beautiful girls grow up.

CHAPTER 11 – ATTACCA, PRESTISSIMO AND PRECIPITANDO

[Attacca: Indicates an immediate move to the next section of music. Prestissimo: Very, very fast. The fastest tempo. Precipitando: Rushing, headlong.]

It is true that time waits on no one. I remember being out doing the grocery shopping one day. My refrigerator and all of the cabinets were missing the basic staples. I wanted to make this a quick trip, so I drove to the store closest to my house. After swiftly selecting my grocery items and paying for them, I headed to the store's exit and proceeded to my car. As I was loading the car, I heard a female store clerk yell, "Ma'am, ma'am". Thinking that there was a problem or perhaps that I had dropped something from my purse, I quickly finished loading my purchases, secured my car, and traveled back toward the store entrance to meet her. Once we were face to face, she stated that the produce manager wanted to speak with me. I asked why would the produce manager need to speak with me, and she responded that he had contacted her on the two-way radio and asked her to deliver his message before I left the store. I thought it was strange, but went back anyway. She walked me over to a man who was short in stature with a strong build -- even the oversized work shirt could not hide his muscles. "Hi" he said, "I'm Mike, the produce manager. Were you looking for something when you were in the produce area?" I told him that I needed potatoes. He replied that there was a delay with the produce delivery; however, he expected it within the hour. With the perishable groceries out in my car, I could not afford to wait on a potato delivery truck; nor could I spare any time to continue to talk. I thanked him for the information and turned in an attempt to exit the store for the second time. He quickly asked for my telephone number. I thought to myself, *"Really – potatoes just are not important to me."* When I turned to look at him, it was obvious that he had much more than potatoes on his mind. Although I hesitated for a moment, I did eventually give him my number, and he promised that I would hear from him very soon.

As promised, he called me within a day's time and we talked for hours. Mike shared that he was a single dad with one son, that he owned his own home, and that he worked hard to provide a solid, stable life for his son. Listening to him talk about his efforts and his son indicated to me that family was important to Mike. We enjoyed talking to each other and he called me at least once every day. Communication with him was non-stop. I liked the way he talked and his confidence; however, if I am completely honest, his muscular physique was very attractive as well. Mike demonstrated a consistent attentiveness that I grew to depend on. After only three weeks of knowing each other, he began to anticipate things that he thought I would need around the house; and progressed to bringing groceries over without me even asking. I thought, at first, that this was an extremely kind gesture; however, what I later learned was that this was all part of Mike's master plan.

After only three months of dating, Mike popped the question. Yes -- THE QUESTION -- he proposed. In hindsight, I realize that he planned the proposal strategically for a time when my entire family would be present -- Christmas morning. He knew from our earlier conversations that my family traditionally met at my parent's house for Christmas breakfast. After breakfast, we would open gifts, play cards, and prepare the Holiday dinner feast. Mike knew that everyone would be light-hearted, high-spirited and full of joy. He relied on the notion that no one would dare say or do anything on that day to ruin the good vibrations felt by all in attendance. He felt confident that if he made a big production of getting down on one knee and proposing to me in front of my entire family, I would not say, "No." I was not ready for this proposal. Our relationship was not ready for marriage, but I would not embarrass him in front of everyone. I would not create an even bigger spectacle on Christmas day. Instead of honoring myself and following my good sense, I said, "Yes," and helped to make the Christmas Day celebration even more exciting.

The days flew by so fast after the proposal that it seemed like the wedding was the following week. On the first day of March, I pulled up to the cemetery to put flowers on Lewin's grave. This time, however, I was coming to tell him that I was getting married that day. I stood at the gravesite talking to Lewin in sprit and telling him about Mike. Before I knew it, an hour had passed and I suddenly I realized that I was late for my scheduled arrival time at the church. When I checked the time, it was half past three. I should have been at Mike's church by 3:00 that afternoon, but the ceremony was not until 5:00. I hurried home and when I arrived, it was nearly 3:45. Mike was sitting outside in his rental car with the engine running. I ran up to the car and quickly apologized for being late. He looked at me and said, "This is supposed to be our day, Carol, and you've spent more than an hour talking to a dead man. Do you want to live in the past with the dead or move forward to the future with the living?" He stared at me so intensely that if his eyes were lasers, he would have burned a whole through my head. He was clearly upset, so I apologized to him and told him, and explained that I was ready to make him my husband. Opening his car door abruptly and causing me to step back, he walked to the passenger side and said with a huge smile, "Well, come on then." Our wedding ceremony was very simple, just a notch up from my first wedding. We had only immediate family in attendance.

CHAPTER 12 – FORTISSIMO, MARCATO AND VIGOROSO

[Fortissimo: Very loud. Marcato: Emphasized, heavily accented. Vigoroso: Vigorous, strong.]

Our marriage got off to what I thought was a good start. I cared so much for him and he seemed so good for my girls. Although, we were still learning one another, it felt like things were progressing nicely. Well, at least that is what I thought. Spring had come, and just as in nature when winter snow melts away and the true colors of spring become visible, Mike's true colors became vividly clear to me. It was a vibrant awakening, but not a beautiful one. Mike's surface glitter and sparkle seemed to melt away as snow does during the spring thaw; and what was uncovered was a man who was **controlling, abusive,** and **selfish**. I am not using these three descriptive words lightly. I did some online research and the definitions of controlling, abusive and selfish definitely apply in this case.

Textbook Definitions:

a) **Controlling**. A controlling man demands what he wants. He criticizes constantly. He tries to isolate you from others. He attaches conditions to his love and affection. He is a master at guilt trips. He constantly snoops and checks up on his partner.

b) **Abusive.** An abusive man verbally and/or physically will usually demonstrate some or all of these signs –

- **He will romance you.** He will seem like he is the most romantic man you have ever met. He will buy you flowers and gifts. He will be attentive while making you feel special and wanted. He will make you feel like you are his entire world — *because he wants your world to revolve around him.*

- **He will want to commit — very quickly.** He will say things like, "…we are made for each other," and how he cannot imagine his life without you. He may call and/or text you constantly and consistently. He will sweep you off your feet, and say he has never loved like this before or this deeply. He will insist on being exclusive right away, and will likely want to move in together, or even get married, very quickly. *He needs you to love him, and to belong to him.*

- **He will want you all to himself.** He will glare at other men for looking at you, and question you about your male friends. He may ask you to change the way you dress or to stop wearing makeup so that you will not garner the attention of other men. He may suspect or accuse you of flirting or cheating. *You may think this jealousy is cute or even loving — at first. However, he will soon make you feel guilty for spending time with friends or family.*

- **He will seem very concerned about you.** He may get upset if you do not call him back right away, if he cannot account for your whereabouts, or if you come home late. He will say it is because he worries about you. He may start to question whom you saw, where you went, and what you were doing. *This is his way of masking his control as concern for your well-being.*

- **He will be sweet and caring — sometimes.** He will be the sweet, loving man who everyone else sees, and who you fell in love with. *However, he will sometimes become the man who puts you down, makes you feel guilty, isolates you, threatens you, and possibly abuses you physically.*

- **He will play the victim.** If there is a problem on the job, it will always be someone else's fault or someone is out to get him. If he is upset, he will somehow blame you for his feelings and actions. He will expect you to make him happy and fulfilled — and when he is not, he will seek to blame you. He may say things like, "I act this way because I love you so much," or "I love you so deeply that it makes me crazy." *Eventually, he will blame you for "making" him want to hit you or for actually hitting you.*

c) **Selfish.** *A selfish man* talks about himself so much that he rarely gets around to asking about you. He ignores or downplays your emotions. He nags about how you look and dress. The smallest things bother him and he seems to argue for no apparent reason. He finds you as the main culprit for everything that goes wrong for him and he truly believes that his behavior is normal. He may lie to make himself appear to be better or more stable. *If you challenge him or call him out on his behavior, he will turn into someone you do not recognize.*

My Real-life Examples of Controlling, Abusive and Selfish Behavior:

A. Mike felt that he could and should be his true self in our marriage; however, I could not be myself. He was a very jealous and selfish man. He did not want me to fix myself up or do anything that would attract attention to me. He did not want anyone else looking at me or making flattering comments. I actually wore a Size Six in clothing; but Mike insisted that I buy and wear a Size Eight and sometimes even Size Ten. He also wanted to have a say in what I wore, and even how I styled my hair.

When Mike got a tattoo with my name and my daughters' names, I was flattered -- initially. At first, I thought it was such a sweet and loving gesture. In hindsight, I see that it was more of a statement, a warning sign to all who saw that tattoo that we "belonged" to him.

B. This man perpetuated a complete fraud. It was not until we were already married that I learned that he did not own his home. He was renting someone else's property, and shortly after our wedding, he had to move into my home. Mike also had major issues with his credit, and it was not long before the dealership repossessed his car. As his wife and helpmate, I used my credit to get another car for him. I thought this was a beautiful demonstration of my love and support for him. On the surface, he seemed appreciative; but under the surface, I believe he was intimidated and viewed my gesture as a blow to his pride. After a while, he treated me as if I did something wrong by getting a car for him.

C. I remember attending an outdoor concert with Mike. At some point, he went to get a drink and while he was gone, I went to the restroom. When he returned with the drink, I had not yet returned from the restroom. When I did return, he accused me of being with someone while he was gone. Of course, I told him that his accusation was absurd. With that, he became physically violent, grabbing me by my throat and choking me. I tried to break free from his grasp but I just was not strong enough to defend myself from his strength and his rage. I could not breathe and I remember gasping frantically for air. I thought I was going to die right there at the concert in front of hundreds of witnesses. Once the people around us noticed what was happening, several men came to my aid and it took several men to pull him off me.

I think a part of me felt sorry for Mike because he was competing with the beautiful memories I had of my love and life with Lewin. In truth, there was no competition because no one could compete with the love I had for Lewin. Mike was attempting to fill a void that was just too big, too deep, and too meaningful. Still, I forgave Mike, I compromised, and I hung in there because I wanted so much to have that "perfect" family that I started building with Lewin. I did not want to give up and admit to failure.

After the aforementioned examples and incidents, the final straw came when I was cleaning out his truck and found a love letter from another woman. As crazy as it sounds, it was not his fists that ran me off -- it was his unfaithfulness. I knew, without question, that I had to get away from him.

This marriage was over! Marriage, as had been told to me, was supposed to be a partnership made with compromise, love, and respect. My marriage to Mike did not consist of any of those qualities. I had overlooked, endured, risen above and denied many things in our accelerated, unsubstantiated relationship; but I was not about to share my husband with another woman. At first, he would not sign the papers. I did not know what to do. I just knew that I wanted OUT! I know that marriage is a sacred covenant, and I know that God ordained marriage; BUT I prayed, and prayed, and prayed that God would make a way to release me from this bondage. Then one day, he finally said, "Okay, Carol, you can have your divorce." I thanked God for letting me get out of that mess and for helping me to realize, early on, that the monster *(I mean Mike)* was not the man for me.

CHAPTER 13 – DA CAPO AND CAPRICCIOSO

[Da Capo: Return to the beginning. Capriccioso: In a whimsical or fanciful style.]

Disappointingly, I found myself back at square one. Falling back into my previous habit, I was going out again and praying that I would find true love. One night, while at a local club, I met my Prince Charming. It was Jazz Night at the club, and I had talked my mother into joining my aunt and I, since the music and atmosphere would be a little more low-key than normal. The mellow vibes flowed through the club like a welcomed breeze on a summer's night. The band finished their last set and thanked the crowd for coming out. The DJ would soon take his place in the booth. I got up to go to the restroom. While washing my hands, I took a quick look in the mirror, made sure my look was intact, and headed back across the dance floor to our table.   As I passed the bar, I felt a tug on my wrist. I looked down at my wrist and allowed my eyes to detect the source of the tug.   There stood a bald, dark-skinned man of average height. I first noticed his smile; it was nice. Then, he leaned in and spoke into my ear. His voice, even over the DJ and club speakers, was like crushed velvet – smooth and richly colored with deep inflections here and there. This man surely had my attention. He went on to tell me that his name was Elton, and he asked, "Would you give me the honor of being my dance partner?"

Acknowledging the nod of my head, he gently pulled my wrist once more and led me out to the dance floor. Frankie Beverly and Maze's tune, "Before I Let You Go" played in the background.   I broke out in a two-step -- almost Chicago style. I did not think he would be able to keep up with me because other than his smile, he did not look like he had it in him *(oh little did I know at that moment and beyond)*.   Elton caught my rhythm within the first eight counts. However, what really got me is when the song got to the part that goes *"...you know I think the sun rises and shines in you, and you know that there's nothing I would not do"* runoff. At that moment, he did his own little special step, came back in, and turned me into a full spin and dip. With that skillful move, he took my breath away, and put a smile on my face that I could not wipe away. We danced on the floor for a few more songs talking through the music. Elton said he was the minister of music at his church and asked what church I attended.   I responded with the name of my church, and was surprised to find that we had a mutual friend. I would have danced with him longer, but I had my mom and aunt with me; therefore, I cut my dance partner loose. We exchanged information and he walked us to our car.

The next day, I received a call from Elton asking me out on a date. I stalled for a moment to think about it. Initially, I thought I should take my time; but then I said to myself, *"He is different -- after all, he is a music minister."* In that same span of a moment, I even reasoned with myself that he could be a good friend, or even possibly the man I had wanted to be in my life and my daughters' lives. I answered, yes; but I set the date for later in the week. We decided on a lunchtime date. When I arrived at the restaurant, I noticed that he was already there and seated. In fact, he had positioned himself where he could see me enter the restaurant. Upon seeing me, he stood up to greet me. He was sporting a freshly shaved head, and was wearing a white button-up shirt and crisp heavily starched jeans. As I arrived at our table, he opened his arms and gave a friendly hug. There was a single red rose on the table. Elton hit me with the classic, corny "a-pretty-rose-for-a-pretty-lady" line. I thought I rolled my eyes discreetly, but he caught it and asked if I disliked roses. I coyly responded, "I like roses just fine. I'm just trying to see if I like them from you." He smiled as if to say, *"Game on"*, and that was really the start of our journey.

From then on, we talked every day; which I thought was a bit unusual, as most men did not talk much over the phone – especially after just meeting someone. When I say we talked, I mean we were engaged in long, full, interesting, thought-provoking conversations. This was not the short, mindless back-and-forth texting with acronyms, symbols, and emojis that passes for conversations today. During our time of getting to know each other, I learned that he was not only the minister of music, but that he was a musician, as well as the lead singer in a band. This was confusing to me, at first; however, Elton seemed to love the Lord as much as I did. I went on to learn many other things about him, like the fact that he was originally from the north and had two children from a previous marriage. Nevertheless, Elton and I started spending more time together. Before I knew it, our dates turned into short road trips where I would travel with him and his band on gigs.

Royal Chocolate was the name of Elton's band. I thought it was a somewhat edgy title being that they also sang gospel music, but their fans had no problem with it. In fact, the crowd loved them. The first concert I attended with Elton was at the Columbia Coliseum in South Carolina. Royal Chocolate was the opening act. Backstage at the venue, the different entertainers walked back and forth in the halls. Whenever they were not walking, they were yelling for one of their people, demanding something or another. Royal Chocolate's members shared a hotel room on the day of their performances to get dressed. Often times, they would just all arrive fully dressed and ready to perform. On one particular night, as the band waited for their introduction, the band members warmed up individually. Some were pulling strings on the guitar, tapping the drumsticks together, and some lightly blew into their horns. Elton even ran through a few vocal cords, and every now and then, he would turn and serenade me. If I recall correctly, someone had told me that all the band members were married, except Elton. This made me feel very special as I sat backstage with the other *wives*. I felt like I was the one; and that God had saved him just for me. Finally, the emcee introduced Royal Chocolate and the band members took the time to kiss their *wives* backstage before going on to perform. Elton gave me a quick kiss before he stepped into position. I watched from the stage right as Royal Chocolate began to play. Elton had not sung a note and the crowd was already rocking. When he finally did bellow out that bravado tenor voice of his, the crowd grew more enthusiastic -- even dancing in the aisles. Their performance slot was only fifteen minutes, but the crowd and I would have loved more.

I was amazed and caught up in the whole experience of the night; and I was delighted when Elton and I headed off to dinner at a nearby bar and grill, without the rest of his band. We sat down and chatted reflectively about the show. Out of nowhere, Elton apologized. When I asked what the apology was for, he replied, "The behavior of my fellow band members." When I asked why he felt the need to apologize about the band members, he replied by saying something about the way his band members were kissing all over those females. I responded by saying, "I don't see anything wrong with them kissing their wives. As a matter of fact, you were being openly affectionate towards me." Elton looked at me over the rim of his glass and said, "None of their wives were at the Coliseum tonight, and definitely not backstage." He appeared to take a large gulp of his drink as to put a period at the end of his sentence. Elton went on for the next 20 minutes or so telling me how the band members were all about the "groupie" life. He explained that while at performances, the band welcomed any random women who made themselves available to the band. The whole conversation shocked me, and immediately began to feel disgusted. I am sure the expression on my face spoke volumes, and when our food arrived, I was no longer hungry. Elton quickly came to his own defense by saying, "That's the kind of mess that they do; but I'm a one-woman man, Carol.

I am looking for a woman that I can build something with -- you know, grow with." He continued with, "I am not made to be in the streets and chasing women. Furthermore, I just want one good woman that I can love, take care of, and make my wife." I felt like he was being genuine, but my mind was going back and forth between Elton's words and what my eyes witnessed. At this point, I did not know what to think of those other members of the band. I just did not know what to take from this situation. From the outside looking in, it was crazy to think about Royal Chocolate members with a different woman every night while their wives were holding things down at home and taking care of their children. Elton even shared that a few of them even had a steady "road wife" a.k.a. mistress. Again, I told myself that Elton was different. I reasoned that he would not tell me all of this if he was also playing an active role in this tawdry, high school player business behavior. I reasoned that he had to be trustworthy and that I was special to him; otherwise, he would not break the *"man code"* by sharing this information.

CHAPTER 14 – INCALZANDO, LEGATO AND COUNTERMELODY

[Incalzando: Getting quicker. Legato: Smoothly. Indicates no break between notes. Countermelody: A vocal part that contrasts with the principal melody.]

Days and weeks passed, as our relationship continued to grow. Our dates became more frequent and my accompanying him to his gigs became a normal thing for us, as well. We even started to visit one another's churches. Still, introducing him to my daughters was something that I had not yet done. A part of me felt as though I would somehow get some type of supernatural nod of approval from above to let me know if Elton could or would be someone to have in our lives. Nevertheless, I did not rush to make any introductions because the relationship was still developing. I had moved entirely too fast in my relationship with Mike, and I was not about to make the same mistakes.

Elton and I moved about in our own little world. I remember us walking into his third concert hand and hand. This is the night that he let me know that I was the one. You see, we both noticed a man wearing a royal blue tailored suit standing off to the side and talking to one of the band members. I could quickly tell that he was checking me out; and Elton would have had to be blind to miss this man's attention towards me. As he scanned me over with his eyes for about the fourth time, he asked Elton, "Who is that?" Elton smiled and pulled me close to his side and replied, "This is Carol -- my lady." It felt good and it was a welcomed changed from previous relationships. "Elton's Lady" – that is who I was from that day forward.

It was as if I was a new Rolex on Elton's arm. It seemed as though he was not trying to button-up or roll down his sleeve to hide all that shine. He made me feel like I really meant something to him. Everywhere we went he would sing my praises, shower me with compliments, and just be the perfect suitor. "This is my lady – Carol," sounded like music to my ears when he would say it. Equally important were the unexpected flower deliveries and the handwritten letters in my mailbox, on my car, and in my shop. The closer Elton came to my front door, the more apparent it became that the time had come for him to meet my girls. Elton was a true charmer, and he won my girls over immediately. When he took all of us out to eat for the first time, it seemed that money was no object. He spoiled my daughters that evening and made them feel as if they were little princesses. Understandably, the girls almost immediately gave their nods of approval for this new man in mommy's life.

Everything seemed to be leading down the path to the picture in my mind of the complete family that I always wanted. Everything seemed just right until my mother called one day and asked me to come to her house. She said she wanted to talk with me about something, and all I could hear was concern in her voice. I wasted no time in going next door, and Mom greeted me and quickly sat me down. She informed me that my friend, Pam, had called her. I interrupted to ask if everything was okay with Pam. I was concerned because I had just seen Pam a few weeks ago, and I had even recently spoken to her over the phone. "Pam is fine," mom replied. She continued on saying that a nurse that works at the hospital with Pam confided that she and Elton had been seeing one another. My mouth dropped, as I was in disbelief. I negated everything my mom just told me and angrily responded, "Why did she call you, when we had just recently spoken? Everybody is so jealous of Elton and me. I just believe that people need to mind their own business!" In a calmer voice, I said, "Mama, he is not seeing anyone else but me." I left my mother's house aggravated to say the least. After arriving home, I immediately called Elton to get to the truth of the matter. When I told him the story that my mom got from Pam, he said that it was crazy. He went on to reiterate that he only wanted to be with me. I told Elton that if he wanted to see other people he could; however, I was not going to participate in a shared relationship. Of course, his response was not good enough. Deep down inside, I knew Pam would not lie to me. Moreover, I knew that she would not involve my mother unless it was true, and she wanted me to get the information from a source I loved and trusted. I wanted and planned to speak with Pam personally; however, with my busy work schedule and family life, I just did not make time to do it. Instead, I found myself praying for clarity. One thing that is for sure, if you pray for an answer, you will get an answer – but maybe not the answer you want.

The whole nurse accusation thing made me back off from Elton for a few days. Before I knew it, it was the weekend. I had spoken to him, but I had kept our calls succinct. On Thursday of the following week, he said that he wanted to prove how serious he was about our relationship. He wanted to take me out of town for the weekend. I thought to myself, "How is this going to prove anything," but I still agreed to go. Riding in the car, I mostly looked out the window wondering what I was thinking by agreeing to come on this long ride with this man. After the first few hours, we stopped for lunch. After the restaurant's female host guided us to our seats, the server came over, greeted us and asked what would we like to order? Elton abruptly stood up and started singing Lionel Richie's, "Once, Twice, Three Times a Lady" at the top of his voice. He continued his tableside performance by grabbing my hand and kneeling at my side of the table serenading me. I was thinking, *"This man is crazy, but I think I am falling for him."* Elton got through the first verse and received a hearty applause from the onlookers and restaurant staff. He ended saying, "Thank you all, but special thanks to this beautiful lady here at my side." Elton also took a moment to inform the crowd that he would soon be performing in their town. After he kissed my forehead and bowed, he sat down. It was that kind of charm and the laughter that kept me believing in Elton and that this was really a true love. His serenade at the restaurant seemed to break the ice. We spent the rest of the drive enjoying one another. The laughing and talking made the long hours to New York bearable. It was late when we reached our destination, so we checked into our hotel room and rested.

The next morning, I awakened to a beautiful day. This would make the short drive from the hotel to his mother's house a carefree trip. We pulled up in front of a two-story Brownstone home and walked up the stoop ringing the doorbell once. The doors soon opened to find an excited mother greeting her son with a hug and a kiss. You would have thought that we had met before because she greeted me the same way. Mrs. Clark welcomed me into her home that day without any hesitation. As we entered the residence, Elton said, "Mama, this is the lady I have been telling you so much about. This is my lady Carol." It appeared that he was hanging on to these words. His mother was a kind and charming woman who placed a high value on family. After we visited with Mrs. Clark for a while, she introduced me to her husband. Mr. Clark was just as pleasant as his wife was. Watching Elton and his parents interact, one would have never known that Mr. Clark was Elton's stepfather. They seemed like a wonderful family unit, and seeing them together made me think that just maybe, Elton could be the right man for me. We spent the weekend with his parents, and I remember envisioning that my girls would experience the same kind of love and sense of family unity if Elton and I were to marry one day.

Also during our short trip, we spent time with his family and friends. They took me on several tours around the city. They wanted to be sure that I had a good experience while being in New York. I saw all of the touristy spots like Wall Street, the Empire State Building, Twin Towers, Central Park, and of course, the fabulously famous stores on 5th Avenue. It was truly an action-packed weekend. I enjoyed meeting his family and friends, and if I was not sure at first, I now knew that Elton planned on us spending our futures together.

Our drive back to Georgia was certainly different from the drive up to New York. Every part of our conversation seemed to be about happy times. It was during this trip home that Elton expressed what I thought was his genuine thoughts and intentions for me. He was telling me the things that he admired in me that were different from what he had seen in other women. Elton seemed to be getting quite comfortable. In fact, he had a set of rules for every situation. Elton even uttered to me the two things that would make him walk away from our relationship -- cheating on him and going out with other people. Of course, I expressed the same two things as being causes that would make me leave him, as well. Maybe, just maybe, Elton had been through some bad relationships that made him feel that he just could not stand to be hurt again. I wanted to believe that he was the man that he described himself to be. I decided at that moment that I would be the one to show him the love that he had been missing. With that thought in the back of my mind, I accepted the compliments, letters, flowers, and gifts as true sentiments of his growing love for me.

CHAPTER 15 – AGITATO, DISSONANCE AND INCANTATION

[Agitato: Agitated, restless. Dissonance: The perceived instability of two or more tones. Incantation: A series of words said as a magic spell or charm.]

L ife was good. Yes indeed, it was good. It was so good that I felt it was time for Elton to meet the rest of my family. Our family reunion was a few months away, and as far as I was concerned, it would be just the right setting for him to meet everyone. We discussed him accompanying my family and me for the reunion, and he was onboard. I could hardly contain my excitement as the date of our family reunion grew near. I just knew that my family would love Elton just as much as I already did.

Our drive to Alabama was a trip of fun and laughter. Elton and my family clicked right away. He did what came natural, which was being the entertainer that constantly captivated the audience. Elton played the piano and sang many songs. He treated the family reunion as though he were on a stage in a coliseum. I remember driving back to Augusta thinking to myself, *"Carol, he is the one."* Undoubtedly, things felt so right that I believed it was time to let Elton spend more time with me and my girls as a family. Elton would take us to the movies, out to eat, swimming, and many other family-oriented activities. I could feel myself putting him into a place that was obviously moving too fast. It was noticeable that Elton loved children; in fact, he had a great relationship with his children. As more time passed, we began to plan family vacations together. We would later go on to take the children on a Disney Cruise, fly out to Las Vegas, and more. At the same time, Elton was making sure that I knew that I was the most important person in his life. He began doing things for me around the house and in the shop. It was nothing for him to move boxes or organize something in the shop before going to his rehearsals.

One day after Elton had worked in the shop, I walked him to the door. We said our goodbyes and I went back in to finish my organizing. Shortly thereafter, the front doorbell rang. Thinking Elton must have forgotten something, I sprinted to the door and quickly opened it smiling and expecting to greet my man once again. Instead of Elton, at my front door stood a tall, brown-skinned woman with what looked like a Curley-Sue wig on her head. "I said," hello how can I help you?" Thinking she needed my professional hair care services and mistakenly come to my front door; I awaited her response. Awkwardly, she attempted to glance over my head as if to peer into my house. Instantly, a chill came over me and I immediately stepped out onto the porch and closed my door behind me. I did not think of my own safety, but more about protecting everyone else who lived under my roof. I asked again, "Is there something I can help you with?" With a blank stare on her face, she asked, "Ma'am was that Elton that just left from here?" In shock, I asked her what business was it was hers. She then proceeded to tell me that she and Elton had been in a relationship for the past several months. This woman went on to say that recently she had sensed that something was going on with him, but she could not quite figure it out; so, she decided to follow him. I told myself, *"This lady is crazy!"* Like a reflex, I became defensive and yelled out, "Elton is my boyfriend! Furthermore, you need to get off my property before I call the police." Without pause, the woman lunged at me getting up close and personal. Through her bitten lip, she snarled, "Tell Elton that his lady stopped by." She then angrily turned and scurried back to her car, which she had parked just beyond my driveway. My heart was racing and my chest was heaving as if I was gasping for air. I ran back into my house and called Elton on his cell phone. He did not answer. Not waiting to hear back, I tried calling him several more times, but it kept going to voicemail. Cradling myself, I could not help but think, *"What if my daughters had been home? "What if that woman became violent?"* She could have come to my front door and shot me point-blank and who would have ever known? "Oh my God," I thought I had stepped into some *Fatal Attraction* scenario. She certainly seemed confrontational. She was brazen enough to come to my front door. Who knows what else she could have done?

I was pacing my floor when the phone finally rang. The moment I answered the phone, he started with, "Baby, I'm so sorry. That girl does not mean anything to me. She is one of the band groupies who has a thing for me." I have told her to leave me alone," Elton said in what seemed to be a single breath. I was so angry about the situation that I just hung up the phone. The thought of a strange woman coming to my door gave me an overwhelmingly sense of alarm. Fifteen minutes later, I heard a banging on my door. I grabbed my phone, went to the door, and yelled out without hesitation, "You better not be back on my property!" "Carol baby, it's me. I just want to explain," Elton wined from the outside. I opened the door, yelling, "Baby! I am not your baby! I am not your lady! I am not your anything! *Curley-Sue* is your lady – I heard it from her own lips." Elton grabbed me and said, "Carol, baby, I promise you that I don't have anything to do with her. She is a stalker, I swear." To that, I erupted with a barrage of statements and questions, "Elton, she must have told you she was here. How else would you have known? Did she come to see you, too? What would have happened if my daughters answered the door? What would we have done if she physically attacked one of us? You have brought mess to my home and to my doorstep." I broke down in tears through my ranting. When he first reached out, I was reluctant to allow him even to touch me. However, being the charmer that he was, I slowly seemed to melt in his arms. The more he talked, the more I listened, and slowly I calmed down.

When I look back on the situation that occurred that day, I should have reminded myself that when you pray, you should expect an answer, and you should be prepared to receive that answer – whatever it is. That woman may have been a little off her rocker by showing up at my house; but honestly, she was the answer to my prayers. I asked God to open my eyes, and not to let me become a victim to my sappy, idealistic emotions. I asked Him to let me see everything I needed to see." However, when He did, I just did not want to see what was staring me right in the face.

Over the next few days, Elton came by daily and worked hard to repair the damage created by the visit of his uninvited acquaintance to my home. He even sought legal advice resulting in a restraining order against Ms. *Curley-Sue*. To my surprise, he included my residence as well as my mother's in the restraining order. Elton went on to file a civil suit for stalking and disturbing the peace against her. In fact, he won the case in court. Elton was making it hard to believe that he could have been seeing her or anyone else for that matter. He checked in with me hourly and even during his rehearsal breaks. He showered me with gifts and flowers every chance he got; and he wrote me love letters that read like sworn pacts of his devotion to me, and to our relationship. I forgave him and decided to move forward with him. I actually talked myself out of the good-sense reasoning that was screaming "RUN" in my ears. Instead, I kept reminding myself that he was a minister of music, he performed in a live band, and he could not help it if loose women, low self-esteemed women threw themselves at him. Why did I not trust what I knew to be true? When I think back on this, I think of Eve in the Garden of Eden. There the serpent slithered up to her telling her all the things she needed and wanted to hear to get her to do the very thing God WARNED her not to do. I would find out later just what a sly, sneaky snake Elton was.

It was spring break and, of course, the children were out of school. With this in mind, I thought it would be a great idea to get all the kids together, his and mine, and go on a trip. When I mentioned this to Elton, he was excited and told his children right away. At the same time, I made an additional request that he arrange for me to meet his children's mother before we departed. He agreed and spoke with his ex-wife, Michelle, who also consented. My only intention was to meet the mother of his kids and make sure she was okay with them being around me. As a mother, my daughters are the most important thing in my life. Therefore, I could only assume the same for Michelle. Therefore, out of respect and putting myself in someone else's shoes, I knew this was a necessity. Not many days passed before our meeting took place. Michelle met us at Elton's place to drop the kids off and to have our sit down. When she came in, I did not know what to expect. Michelle sat down and was completely genuine. Elton took the kids to grab lunch while we talked. I told her what my intentions were with Elton and their kids. In contrast, Michelle told me about her connection with Elton. She went on to say that her only tie with him was their children. In fact, she stressed that they were all that mattered to her. With that, we sat and chatted about everything but Elton and our kids. Michelle left me with her blessings to be in her children's lives. The next week, the six of us loaded up heading on to a trip designed to see how we would all bond. Our four children were all around the same age. Ashley was two years older than his son was; yet, his son's birthday was the day after Francis' birthday. Elton's daughter was only one year younger than Francis was. The kids sat in the back of the vehicle talking and playing as if they had known one another for years. During our vacation, they seemed to grow closer and so did Elton and I. I admit there was nothing but good thoughts running through my mind as I watched everything unfold. We had a whole week of just us -- no work, no phones, no distance, just he and I, and our family.

Back home with everyday life, things were going great. There were no problems, but I should have known by now that there is always calm before the storm. Elton was juggling his personal life with the girls and I, as well as with his band. Royal Chocolate had a concert coming up. They were going to have total control over it. They had printed up flyers and had put the word out in their circles, but there were issues. The week before Royal Chocolate's concert Elton's worries, which he tried to bury inside, rose to the surface. He was becoming a little snippy. He had been picking up the girls for me from time to time when I was busy in my salon. On this particular day, I called him and asked if he would mind picking them up. He said he would do it. When I finished work, I began to prepare the sauce for the pasta dish I planned for dinner. When it was time to cook the pasta, I realized that I was out of pasta noodles. I called Elton and asked him to stop and get a box of pasta for me. He snapped, "I'm not your errand boy." Wounded by his response, I told him just to forget about it and he hung up the phone. Of course, this very quickly caused my attitude to change for the worse. Despite Elton's response, he did come with the noodles; but he did not try to conceal his perturbed attitude as he handed the box of pasta to me. As I took it, I could not help but tell him how his snippiness made me feel. After listening, Elton apologized. He told me that he felt stressed because the concert ticket sales were down. He believed that the poor ticket sales were due to a lack of community support. Elton said that if the sales did not pick up soon, the band would have to consider canceling the concert.

Putting my hurt feelings and emotions aside, I told him not to worry, and that things would come together. I had him give me some tickets to sell. That night, I made a sign and put it up in my salon. The wording on the sign read, "Get your Royal Chocolate concert tickets here." Throughout the week, I sold tickets to my customers. On the positive side, word of the concert and the tickets began to spread. Day by day, people were coming to the salon to purchase tickets. Some of the people I had never met in my life. Before long, I had sold them all. I did not have hundreds of tickets, but when Elton came by that night; I handed him the envelope with the money in it. As a result, he lifted me up and spun me around. He was so grateful! When he arrived at work that night, he sent an email thanking me for helping him with the ticket sales. He also apologized again for his snippy attitude.

The night of the concert Elton asked if I would handle the door. That meant me sitting at the door and greeting people as they entered the club. As I sat there, I saw all of the people to whom I had sold tickets within the last week. Royal Chocolate's fan base had not failed them; the club was packed. There seemed to be a common conversation amongst the women that were entering the club. They all freely verbalized their plans for each band member. These plans entailed what they wanted to do and to whom. More than all of the names of the band members, Elton's name seem to chime the most. There was so much chatter about Elton. I did not say a word or allow it to get me flustered because I knew where Elton spent his time and with whom – ME! We were combining our two families to make one whole one. Because I worked the front door, I did not get to see the concert that night; however, a few of my friends were amongst the crowd. They told me that Elton was a little more fresh and flirtatious than normal. Apparently, Elton was singing to a woman in the front row and rubbing her face. If my friends had not been there, I would not have known.

When they told me, I just brushed it off and refused to give it any value. After all, he was an entertainer and that is what they did to ensure a good show. I told myself that it was all part of the act. At least, that is what I thought.

Have you ever thought you were living the perfect life or even a perfect moment? I felt that way every day around Elton. We meshed so well. He was there for me and I was there for him. We had one another's back. When it came to my girls, he would do anything in his power for them. Elton had a busy life. In fact, he worked the third shift during the week at the county jail. He filled his weekends with the church choir on Sundays and with his band on Fridays and Saturdays. On weekday evenings, he had rehearsals with the band. It seemed he had no time for himself. I did not have many complaints because he would be with me during the daytime when I had down time from the salon. Our lives were a little hectic with his schedule, me running my salon, and having my girls who were developing into teenagers. Nevertheless, we were growing closer from day to day. Elton had been spending his extra time at the house with the girls and me; which meant he barely spent any time at his own home. Dating me and managing his other personal responsibilities consumed his schedule. One day we were planning to go catch a movie, but Elton remembered that he needed to do laundry and prepare his uniform for work. I told him to bring the laundry to my house and I would take care of it for him.

I remember something so special happening on one Sunday. The four of us had returned from church and we had an early dinner. As it had become the norm, thoughts of how life could be if we were a family were flowing through my mind. I remember sitting quietly as I watched Elton get dressed for work. As if reading my mind, he caught my reflection in the mirror and turned to me saying, "Carol you know I love you and I love Ashley and Francis, too. I wish that I could be here every day." I smiled, kissed him, and went into the kitchen to pack snacks for his late-night shift. As I lay in my bed later that night, thoughts of what it would be like to have him around all the time flooded my mind. Even though Elton had been saying for months that he planned to make me his wife, something inside was still telling me to get to know him better. Therefore, I decided no matter what, I would give myself time before I said, "I do" again.

Before I knew it, it was our dating anniversary. Not an official anniversary acknowledging the day we met or when the day we became officially a couple, because those dates were constantly in debate. We agreed to commemorate the date of our first date as our anniversary. The date of this anniversary fell during a weekday. Elton decided that we should celebrate by going back to the local Applebee's restaurant. Sitting down to dinner, we were sharing casual conversation when he asked, "Do you think we could live together?" I told him I was not going to be shacking up and playing wife to anyone. He started laughing and said, "You been doing my laundry, cooking for me, helping with the band, and being there for me and my kids when you can. What do you think you have been doing all this time?" I was not sure where he was going with his question, but I replied by saying, "I have been showing you that I care for you and that I am here for you." His retort was, "Exactly Carol! This is why I cannot understand your reasoning for not wanting to live together." "That is not going to work for me, Elton," was all I could muster myself to say. I could feel myself becoming agitated. "Okay Carol, do you want some dessert?" he asked. "Dessert -- not really," I responded dryly.

"Come on," he said, 'I'll order something for you." Elton seemed to have been ignoring my emotions as well as my words. He went on to call the server over and ordered a Blondie Brownie. I rolled my eyes thinking this man is crazy asking me *"what did I think I had been doing all this time."* As far as I was concerned, the real question was *"What had he been doing for the past several months?"* While I busy tossing these thoughts around in my mind, Elton smiled and attempted to charm and joke his way out of this catastrophe of an anniversary. The server approached to the table holding a dessert and announced, "Blondie." Elton, still smiling, responded to the server, "You can put it in the center of the table." I did not take my eyes off him. I could feel anger start to bubble inside of me and I did not even notice the dish that the server placed in front of us.

"Carol, I love you, I really do, and you have been the best thing that has ever happened to me. Do you think you could see being with me forever?" His words slightly lightened up the grim look on my face, and the grim outlook I had of the evening. Elton got up from the table and got down on one knee, and began to sing a little snippet of, *"Once, Twice, Three Times a Lady."* After singing, he looked up at me and said, "Carol I want you to know how I feel. I also want to make sure you know that I am here for you. Furthermore, I want to give you all that you have given to me, and more. Carol, would you be my wife?" As he asked, he motioned his hand towards the dessert that I now saw was an Applebee's Blondie, but the garnishment was a sparkling diamond ring. When I saw it and realized what he was doing, tears of joy flowed from my eyes. "Will you marry me, Carol," he asked again? "Yes," I said through my tears. Our server, a few other servers, and patrons clapped when they heard my response. They had all been watching the whole time. Elton pulled me out my seat by one hand and placed the ring on my finger. He then lifted me up into his arms. Our lips met in a kiss that I can remember to this day. His act of passion made the applause even louder. We were officially engaged to be married!

I was so happy! When we got home, I told my family first. The girls were excited. My mom said she thought he was a nice man; and my dad smiled saying, "That smooth- talking northerner finally made his move." Everyone was happy for us and glad to hear the news -- well, almost everyone. My sister, Angel, still had her reservations about Elton. It did not matter that it was Elton -- she probably would have reservations about anyone that I considered marrying. Although I am older than she is, she is very protective of me. Noting the sound of concern in her voice, I assured her that I would take my time this go round.

Before I started spreading our good news, with anyone outside of our families, I talked with Elton and told him I wanted us to live together for a year before we got married. Much to my surprise, he agreed. At the same time, I had to consider the space that the four of us would be occupying. The girls were growing up and needed more space, and considering that Elton was a musician, we would definitely need additional space for his piano and other equipment. I just was not sure if my house was large enough for all of us. This led me to hire a contractor to survey my property, and draw up some plans for an addition. The contractor offered a fair price for the renovation; therefore, I accepted his offer and scheduled the project to start immediately. Elton's apartment lease expired prior to the completions of my home renovation, so he moved in with the girls and me a little earlier than expected. We had been spending so much time together that his transition to our home was seamless.

Settling into our new living arrangements, we began to plan our wedding. I thought everything was going great; but as always, there was a storm cloud brewing. My father had a doctor's appointment and my mom accompanied him. Dad had been visiting the doctor more frequently, but it did not seem like a cause for concern. My dad had been in a health battle for more than a year, and none of us knew it. At that appointment, the doctor told my parents that he recommended that my dad start chemotherapy within the next 30 days. My mom said her mouth dropped open immediately. An entire year had passed and neither she nor any of us knew what my dad was experiencing. His fight for health had been a lonely one. Within months of the news and before any of us could come to terms with it, my dad passed away. Though we were all hurt and saddened by this loss, I believe my daughter, Francis, took it the hardest. Her grandfather had always been the constant father figure in her life. He enjoyed taking her to annual father-daughter dances, telling her bedtime stories, and just giving her the love that she likely longed for in the absence of her father. God knows that we wish we could have had more time to spend with my father. However, we were grateful for the time that we did have. In the end, we knew he loved us all. Struggling to get through the grieving process, I had to take comfort in knowing that he wanted us to remain strong, and he did not want us to worry or to see him suffering.

Life was certainly different without my father. Little things that do not seem to hold much significance seemed like major losses now. I thought about our loss more and more, and how deeply it affected my life and my children's lives.

This was supposed to be a happy time in my life – a time when I would have loved planning the father-daughter dance for my wedding reception. However, God had a different plan for my dad, and I had to learn once again to lean to God's understanding, and not my own.

CHAPTER 16 – IN UNISON

[Unison: A piece or part of a piece might require playing in unison, where multiple musicians would have to play the piece together. In perfect agreement.]

Our wedding day quickly arrived. It was a beautiful, sun-shiny day in May, and it seemed that everything was in bloom in the Garden City. The Georgia weather on this day in May gave way from its normal hot humid temperature to resemble that of a day in early spring. I had planned every detail to a "T" with some help from Elton. I woke up that morning filled with pure excitement for our big day. In fact, this was the first time, in a long time, when I strictly focused on me. Many of my family members saw me off as I left for the church. They had come from near and far, and it made me feel as though we were having a family reunion all over again. The family welcomed and needed this happy gathering, since we had recently buried my father. Finally, happy times were here again. Driving up to the church seemed more like a dream. Our family was finally becoming the unit that I had longed for. All of the people involved with the wedding were there. I was quickly ushered into the bridal suite so that Elton would not see me. As my bridesmaids and I were in the church suite getting ready, my oldest sister, Cheryl, began to talk to me about married life. She went on to tell me that she was so proud of me. As I received assistance to get into my wedding gown, I had a brief moment of reflection regarding my journey. Getting to this to point certainly was not easy; however, God had seen me through -- just as He promised in His word. In that moment, I smiled and thanked God for being with me, for not leaving me, for keeping me, and for giving me strength.

On cue, the music began to play. It was time to open the doors of the church. The pastor and the groom walked in from the back to take their rightful places up in the front of the church. Immediately following, my eight bridesmaids, to include all three of our daughters and my sister, Angel, began to walk into the sanctuary. Angel had come home from the military to be my maid of honor. Once the flower girls took their positions, the music changed. That was my cue to begin reciting a poem that I had written for our special occasion. At the end of my poem, it was time for my mom to escort me down the aisle. We did not choose any of the music traditionally chosen for a bridal procession, and certainly not the *"Here Comes the Bride"* melody, because Elton wanted to sing a song in which he wrote especially for the occasion. His song was, by his description, a profession of his devotion to me and to our union. When I stepped into the doorway, all eyes were on me. I was wearing a slim cut, laced-topped, V-neck, A-line gown, with full-length lace sleeves, a knee split, and a train. Slowly and gracefully, my mother and I sauntered down the aisle to the altar to the music of Elton's composition. I was trembling a little with nervousness, but my husband-to-be did not appear to be as nervous as I was. After all, he was accustomed to performing in front of large crowds. When I reached the altar and we were face to face, Elton began to sing. The entire ceremony is a vivid memory to me. That day, I smiled so hard that my facial muscles almost went into paralysis.

The reception was even better than the wedding. The décor consisted of ice sculptures, Chiavari chairs, elegant and statuesque centerpieces of fresh cut flowers, crisp linens, soft lighting, and so much more. We also had a live band. Everything was beautiful and moving along perfectly. When all eyes were on us for the first dance, Elton respected my feelings and danced in a way as not to bring about too much attention. He was so smooth. At the time in the reception when the bride traditionally danced with her father, and the groom with his mother, Elton had already planned for things to go seamlessly. He danced with his mother, my mother, and our girls as I watched in loving admiration. He even got his father to help him partner dance with these significant females in our lives. This exhibit of thoughtfulness made me love him even more.

Not long after we had eaten and gotten on the dance floor, Elton somehow got the microphone in his hands and soon joined in singing with the band. No, this was not his band, but one would have thought it was. It was the wedding of my dreams with the exception of my dad's absence. I had everything I had ever wanted in that moment. I can truly say that I was happy the day that I said, "I do" to Elton.

Our wedding day carried on into the night, and after an entire day of festivities, we checked into a local hotel to consummate our marriage. Morning came too quickly. We both wanted to just lay there and bask in the glory of the previous day. As with most hotels, checkout time was 11:00 a.m., and we needed to get home before we embarked on our honeymoon trip. After checking out of the hotel, we drove home to pick up our luggage and head to the airport. We had a mid-day flight scheduled to Jamaica. The flight to Jamaica was quite nice because it was neither long nor tiring. Upon arriving at our honeymoon destination, we noted our chauffeur stood in his professional dress holding a sign. *"Wow,"* I thought! The sign read, Mr. and Mrs. Mayweather. I felt like a celebrity. Everywhere we turned, people were serving us. We had drinks, music, food, doors opened, and all the attention we could have imagined. Equally important, our hotel suite at the Sandals Jamaica Resort for our weeklong stay was remarkable. The staff left no stone unturned. When we opened the doors to our suite, we found the bed adorned with white silk sheets, on top of those sheets were fragrant rose petals. Our eyes zoomed in on the large Jacuzzi tub encircled with scented candles. The refrigerator was abundantly loaded with snacks, and there was a fully stocked, in-room bar. The hotel lobby and grounds were equally as spectacular as our suite. In the lobby's lounge was a beautiful grand piano. Of course, it was not a trip without Elton connecting with his favorite thing to do. Once he discovered the piano, the rest was history. Every night, he sang to the crowd. Oh how he loved the attention of an audience. One would think that I would have become annoyed with this behavior; however, we gained many friends on our trip. So much so, that our newly found friends and us decided to return to the same vacation destination for our 10-year anniversaries. Even with all of the magic of this honeymoon trip, we both missed and often thought of the children, and the importance of their happiness to our union. Before we left Jamaica, we had already made plans for our first "official" family unit vacation. We decided on Florida as our destination, and scheduled the trip to begin days after we were to return home from our honeymoon.

The days of traveling had ended. The kids were back to their normal activities, and Elton and I returned to work. We quickly realized that love did not pay the bills. Our work schedules were not normal for newlyweds. Elton worked at full-time night job during the weekdays. His work schedule was 11:00 o'clock at night until 7:00 o'clock in the morning. In addition to that, his band played and practiced most weekends. To make up for our missing time together, I would travel with him to his engagements. Before I knew it, we had been married for nearly two years and it was not a regular practice for us to sleep in bed together at night – our schedules did not afford us that opportunity. The only exceptions were some holidays, during travel, on vacations, or when Elton took time off from work. Unfortunately, this had become our norm. When we did get the opportunity to sleep together, I made the most of it. It was nothing for me to have candles burning and soft music playing in the background, or to wear a little piece of silk or lace lingerie. Those occasions were not for T-shirts or flannel pajamas; and a headscarf was simply out of the question on those special nights. Elton had let me know early in our relationship that he did not like to look at headscarves while in the bed. Yes, I made the most of those unique occasions. I went all out. I gave it my best. I developed the mindset that when I came to bed, I could make the holiest man's mouth water.

This was my third marriage and I believed the old adage that says the third time is a charm. Moreover, I was determined to make it so. I knew who I was, knew what I wanted, and believed I knew what I needed to do to keep my man happy. Marriage could not be anything but good this time. I did everything that I knew a wife should do. I was both the classic and the modern wife at the same time. I did not let anything slip, to include keeping up the habits that I had started while we were dating. As the classic wife, I cooked, cleaned, and took care of the children. As the modern wife, I worked and paid half the bills. Additionally, I kept myself up -- styled my hair, maintained my weight, dressed nicely, and wore lingerie to bed. Shucks, I even joined his church to make sure that we were getting the same guidance in our faith.

In the meantime, Elton was striving to make changes that would seemingly benefit our new family. He had applied for a supervisory position, which meant he would be able to be on daytime shift, and be at home with me at night. I was too excited! Weeks had passed without word on the status of the new position. We talked about his concerns and I reassured him that he deserved the promotion. In fact, I told him that without a doubt, he was the best officer at the prison; and I knew they would be calling him any day about the promotion. Well that any day turned to two months. Our home phone finally rang two months from the date of his interview. I was working in the salon and once he ended the call, Elton walked in with his head hung low. Seeing the expression on his face, I was worried and quickly inquired why his demeanor was so dismal. He said, "The job just called." I stopped shampooing my client's hair and walked to him with open arms. "Baby, what did they say?" I asked. In a low voice, he said, "My supervisor said that the other candidate ... the other candidate couldn't touch me girl!" He raised his voice and broke out into a dance. We celebrated his promotion and looked forward to this new chapter.

Things changed so fast. Unfortunately, I cannot say they changed for the better. The initial thing that changed was our sleeping arrangement. The first few weeks were great lying together as husband and wife. At the same time, the arguments started. Elton's cell phone rang at all times of the night. His new position required him to answer the calls and respond to all messages. My salon hours began at 6:00 o'clock in the morning and on the salon's busiest days, I could be on my feet for 12 or more hours. Not to mention, I was still ensuring that I cooked dinner by 7:00 o'clock p.m., that I finished the laundry, that the house was clean, and that my family was cared for. Elton had adjusted to his new job, new schedule, and the change of sleep time better than I had. He was accustomed to being awake throughout the night. At midnight when I was ready to shut down for the day, he would want to stay up with the television on sometimes until 2:00 or 3:00 o'clock in the morning. On the contrary, I was not accustomed to that, and my schedule would not allow such. I tried numerous times to find a way to work this out so that my husband and I could remain in the same bed together. For example, I asked him to change the phone setting from ringer to vibrate. He would respond that he could not hear the phone if it only vibrated. In an effort to compromise, I asked if he would place the phone under his pillow. To that, he responded, "Get over it." I went on to ask him if he would turn down the volume on the TV, at least. He responded by saying, "It is not that loud; plus, I cannot hear the TV over your snoring." Until Elton, no one had ever told me that I snored. After two months of the late-night phone calls and messages, blaring television programs, and an excessive lack of sleep for me, Elton decided that he would sleep in another room. This gave the appearance of the perfect solution for both of us. He had his own man cave and we would "choose" to sleep together when we wanted to. It seemed a bit unconventional, but I chose to think positive and see this as a way to keep the marriage fresh and exciting – at least, that is what I thought would happen.

As the years rolled on, Elton started to travel more frequently. For the first five years of our relationship, I always tried to be by his side for out-of-town performances. I never wanted to miss a date. I recall one instance when Royal Chocolate being booked for a show that Elton said was going to be in Chattanooga. Since Chattanooga, Tennessee was not that far away, I decided to travel with Elton, and to allow my now teenage daughters to stay home by themselves. I hurriedly packed an overnight bag. The morning of the trip, I threw my bag in Elton's truck before I headed out to run some last-minute errands. When I returned, Elton was waiting for me, and wasting no time, we hit the road. As we drove, I noticed that we were not following the signs to Tennessee, but to Savannah. "Honey, I thought we were going to Chattanooga?" I questioned. To my question he replied, "Nah, I made a mistake on the itinerary, so we do not even have to stay overnight." "Oh," I said, "I have my bag in the back and everything. I guess I can tell my mom that I will be back sooner than expected." I was about to call my mother on my cell phone, but decided to wait until we actually got back on the road. As I put my phone back in my purse, I saw Elton trying to read a text message. Without hesitation, I said, "You know it is not safe to read messages while you are driving." In response to my statement, he snapped, "Carol, you just sit over there and enjoy the ride."

Throughout the ride, little, nick-picky arguments seemed to come about frequently, actually one after the other, and it seemed without cause. Those little arguments made the two-hour drive feel like 10 hours. We arrived in Savannah without incident. Royal Chocolate was one of the opening acts for an outdoor concert. Once the band checked in with the vendor manager, they were on the stage within the hour and had finished after a 30-minute set. The outdoor venue was great! As a result, Elton decided that we should stay around for a while before heading back to Augusta. We mixed and mingled with the crowd as we had always done when we traveled. There was only one thing different. This time, Elton was introducing me as his "lovely wife". On the drive back, I remember just looking at my husband. I was happy to have shared in this experience with him. The ride home seemed shorter than the drive there, probably because I had fallen asleep. I had awakened to Elton's voice saying, "Bye, I'll talk to you later." Seeing him on the phone reminded me that I had forgotten to call my mother.

"Hey, Sleepy Head," was what my husband said to me as he laid his phone on his lap. Stretching, I smiled at the sound of his voice, asking him how far we were from the house. He said we were about 30 minutes from home. I figured I would just call my mother when I got in. We pulled up to the house and I noticed that the house was strangely dark inside. I knew my girls would not be sitting in the dark. I wondered if Ashley and Francis had gone over to Mom's house. From the door, we could hear music playing loudly. We walked into the dark house. Only the glow of the television gave light to the living room as the music blasted. "What the hell!" I screamed, "Ashley, Francis!" My eyes wanted to bleed seeing both of my daughters, each wrapped up with some boy and necking up on my sofa. Seeing Elton and I, the boys jumped up and ran. "Yeah you better run," yelled Elton. Jogging after them, he blurted out, "You better not let me catch you around here again!" Deadlocking eyes, throwing daggers at my two once innocent little angels, made me quickly park on Reality Street. My daughters were turning into what old folks would describe as fast-tailed, hormonal, teens. I dealt with them swiftly, but I felt the weight of regret and worry fall on my shoulders. I wondered if this was the first time that they had invited boys over to our home. From the looks of what I witnessed, I knew it was not their first times kissing. I thought back to Lewin and me necking in the park, and sneaking around and making a baby. I never regretted having my daughters, but I knew that I did not want them to find themselves being teen moms. I had to make some changes.

Where did the time go? When did my precious little girls become interested in pubescent teenage boys? It was an eye-opening, difficult experience – but necessary for me to see so that I could better focus my attention, and adjust some of my priorities. I guess I will always see them as my little girls.

Ashley was always a sweet and obedient child. I only had to tell her to do something once, and she would listen. She was caring, loving, sensitive, and very, very dainty. Ashley loved playing with her baby dolls and her Barbie dolls. She studied ballet for 10 years, and I thought she was quite good at it. My father and Lewin's father would attend each recital and ensure she received flowers. As she approached her teenage years, Ashley became more of a "people pleaser" and some of her friends took advantage of her sweet nature. Because of that, she resorted to spending more time alone and that caused me to worry – a lot. Physically, Ashley is stunning. Many people say that she looks like me because of our pecan brown complexions; however, she actually has her dad's tiny lips and pointed nose. Emotionally, she is lovable and quite conservative. I think Ashley's personality is more like mine.

My dear Francis was a sweet child, as well; but she was more headstrong. If I told her to go left, she would go right. She believed in doing things her way and was never afraid to take chances. Francis was very outgoing. She loved to have fun, and liked surrounding herself with lots of friends. Like her older sister, she loved playing with baby dolls and Barbie dolls; and she studied Ballet -- but only for five years. Francis really had a special bond with my father. He was the father figure in her life. With us living right next door, my dad would pick Francis and Ashley up from school sometimes. He was great about visiting their school on Grandparents' Day. Physically, Francis is a gorgeous girl. She mostly favors me because she has my lips and nose; but because she has her father's fair skin, everyone says she looks like Lewin. Emotionally, she is a little stubborn and a free spirit.

Several weeks and several Royal Chocolate performances had passed. On this particular week, the band scheduled a performance at a local club. I had already missed four of their bookings, and this would be my fifth. I figured Elton understood. However, I soon learned that he did not. It was as though we had never had a conversation as it related to parenting and the girls. I had to explain to my husband, once again, that the priority for me was to be at home with the girls, especially since their "making out" incident. At first, Elton acted as though he was in total agreement; then, there were times when I felt he tried to use my decision against me. As we all began to adjust to this change, life suddenly took another turn. Elton received a call one day from Michelle, telling him that she was having trouble with their son, Eddie. Elton ended the phone call, shared the details of their conversation, and stated that he needed to bring Eddie to our home to stay. Since family is all-important with me, I was fine with opening our home to Eddie. We decided to make the computer room his bedroom. Eddie was a quiet, modest child who did not know what to expect with his new living arrangement. You see, he did not want to leave his mother; however, they were not getting along. Growing accustomed to his new living arrangements did not have anything to do with growing closer to his daddy. In fact, the girls were very instrumental in him coming out of his shell. The kids went out together, shared things, and formed a real sibling bond. It made me very happy to see how they interacted with each other. In an effort to ensure Eddie felt like a part of us, everyone from my sisters, my mom, and my friends, welcomed and accepted Eddie as a part of the family.

CHAPTER 17 – COMODAMENTE AND DIMINUENDO

[Comodamente: Comfortable and easy. Diminuendo: Gradually decreasing in tempo and intensity.]

E ddie stayed with us for his 8th grade year. During the year, he focused on his schoolwork and kept the lines of communication open with his mother. We knew that he missed being at home with her, but the distance helped him to realize his mistakes and learn to respect his mother's authority. Once things got better and Eddie was on a good path, he moved back home. He completed his sophomore and junior school years at home with his mother; then joined us again for his senior school year. It seemed like our time as parents, at least as over-seeing parents, was ending. On the other hand, the reality of parenting was not and could never be totally over.

Everyone had a plan. Ashley was settling into her own place, attending college, and working. After graduation, Eddie planned to go directly into the Army; and Francis had plans to attend college in Miami, Florida. We admired and appreciated that they were making plans for their futures; but we still had our hands on them figuratively. It was our plan to listen more, offer advice only when asked, and *try* to let them be the *adults* that they thought they were.

The time of our long-awaited empty nest was just around the corner! For so long, it seemed as though we would never get there. Ashley, Francis, and Eddie had all graduated high school leaving just one more child to walk across the stage. Elton's daughter, Donna, was a sophomore high school student, so we knew that her mom would soon know the freedom that we were anticipating. It was time for celebrating! Francis and Eddie graduated on the same day. We would always remember this day because it was also our fourth wedding anniversary. Graduation was on a Thursday morning; and by that evening, we were gone. Elton and I had booked a trip to Myrtle Beach to celebrate our freedom. Somehow, as it was becoming a pattern, this time could not just be about us. Elton had actually scheduled a gig, and we had to stop there first. The ever supportive wife, I actually enjoyed accompanying him to the gig; I really enjoyed being out with my husband once again; and it was refreshingly carefree since we did not have to worry about checking in with the kids or wonder what they were doing. I took advantage of this newfound freedom where I could eat, drink, and be merry.

Later that summer, Elton and I assisted Francis on her move to Florida. It was a milestone occasion for Francis, and for the entire family. It did my heart good to see Elton doing the things that I had envisioned Lewin would do with the girls once they were all grown up. After a few days in Florida, handling Francis' business affairs, and ensuring that she had everything she needed, we headed back to Augusta. Although I had looked forward to us having the house to ourselves, it took a few weeks for me to get used to the silence of being alone in the house all day. Once I became comfortable with this new daily home environment, I remember feeling quite comfortable dreaming about the new life that Elton would now be able to live.

It was not long before my comfort seemed to turn into agitation. It seemed that without the children to be concerned about, we just could not get into a spontaneous, loving rhythm. More times than not, we could be in the house at the same time, but usually in different rooms. Elton spent a great deal of time in the computer room and he always seemed engrossed with whatever he was doing in there. I remember once having the bright idea to try to lure him away from the computer through enticement. I put on one of my sexiest pieces of lingerie, sprayed on my favorite fragrance, sashayed into the computer room, and struck what I thought was a tempting pose. Elton looked at me and said, "You always pick the wrong time to want to be intimate." Since I did not know when the right time was, I tried this ploy several times hoping each time that it would be the right time. It seemed that there was no right time so eventually, I stopped trying to persuade him to make love to me.

I missed the spontaneity that we once shared. The easy, fun, frisky times. I missed spending quality time with my husband and feeling the warmth of his hands and body against my body as we pleasured each other. I was not concerned about anything extramarital. I felt that my husband's responsibilities had him spread entirely too thin. He was a full-time employee at the prison. He was the Minister of Music at his church, which meant weekly choir rehearsals and playing for multiple services at church on Sundays. He was the front man and a musician for Royal Chocolate, which also meant weekly rehearsals and traveling to gigs on the weekends. There were just so many things for Elton to do, and just not enough time to do them all. We both realized that in order for Elton to have the type of musical success that he craved, we both would have to make serious sacrifices. What I understood in my head and what I felt in my heart were not in harmony. One would not think it possible to miss someone who lives under the same roof, but that was my experience.

I started giving him time and space to get some "rest". I did not think he was avoiding me -- I really only thought that he was just extremely tired. It seemed that we spent less and less time together. I suggested to Elton that we go to marriage counseling with his pastor; however, Elton said, "No." I realize now that he did not want any discussion to come up in the counseling sessions that would reveal the true Elton to his pastor. At this point, we did not even worship together anymore. At the beginning of our marriage, I moved my church membership to Elton's church; however, after a while I missed my church family and the style of worship of my church home. I eventually transferred my membership back to my own church. At least there, I could enjoy friendship, fellowship, and faith.

It was around this time that Elton began to pick up more and more gigs. I had less time with my husband and entirely too much idle time to myself. Making money and gaining fame seemed to be his only priority in life. I did not feel like I had a place on his list of priorities. I rationalized that this was just a rough patch or dry season that we were experiencing in our marriage. This man was exhausted and doing everything he could to "make it" in the music performance industry. I decided not to complain; but rather to support his music and career goals, thinking that once he "made it" he would not have to work so hard.

One day, I decided that I needed to get a life for myself — one that did not revolve around the children or around Elton for that matter. A client suggested that I attend a local line dancing class, so I said I would try it. It was as though the Lord knew what I needed — a sisterhood, laughter, physical exercise. I started out with one day per week; and as I learned more dances and met more people, I began to attend classes two and sometime three nights per week. In my mind, I was doing something healthy and wholesome; but of course, Elton saw this as a threat. I would accompany the women from line dance class to local parties and dances where we would hit the dance floor and perform the dances that we learned in class. We all had matching T-shirts and sequined tops that we would wear for special performances. We posed for pictures together and some of us shared our photos on Facebook. We were becoming quite popular and had even booked a few small gigs of our own. It was good, clean fun; many of the women were married; and we all looked out for each other. For whatever reason, Elton had to find fault with it. It seemed that he did not like the fact that I was meeting people, making new friends, and learning to enjoy myself independently. It is a beautiful feeling to have people genuinely like and care about you for no other reason than being your authentic self. That is what I found through the women in my line dance class.

One day at class, my friends surprised me with a birthday celebration. There was a delicious cake and even some gifts. It was one of the best days and I felt loved and appreciated. When I arrived home with the gifts and the remainder of the cake, Elton instantly questioned why these women would do something special for me. Instead of being happy that I was doing something positive, uplifting, and enjoyable, he worked overtime to scandalize it. He eventually stooped to the lowest possible level and called me gay. He called me, the woman who tried in vain countless time to entice him and lure him away from whatever he was doing on the computer, gay! To make a bad situation even worse, Elton flat out accused one of my friends of being gay. He said, "The word on the street is that your friend is gay, and some of the photos you have taken with her are rather suspect." At first, I laughed it off and thought he was being ridiculous; however, he did not stop there. Elton would say all kinds of horrible things to me as though he was trying to provoke me, and to get some type of confession out of me. His statements were unworthy of a response, certainly unworthy of a defense, and I was proud that I let nothing that came out of his mouth stop me from dancing and fellowshipping with my new friends. I understand now that the sisterhood that I formed was certainly there to fill the voids that would later develop.

As long as I was involved in line dance, there was always a party to attend. One great fact about line dancing is that you do not have to have a partner. I began going out to parties and dances with my line dance sisters to fill the void I felt. It was so much fun at first; however, it soon became quite difficult for me. I was growing tired of getting dressed up and attending parties with my friends, as if I was a single woman. It was hard for me to see other couples out enjoying the evening together. Even though many friends surrounded me, I still felt alone inside. I wanted, needed and craved my husband's presence and touch.

Like a ship lost at sea, it seemed that our marriage was now beginning to take a path of its own. Soon, no day of the week seemed off limits for Elton's gigs. Most of the gigs seemed to be in Columbia, SC, and I remember jokingly saying to him that he could have a secret family there because of his frequent visits. On too many occasions, he did not even bother to come home after his gigs in Columbia, SC. I knew that singing was his passion; I considered that he would be tired after performing and packing up the gear; and I trusted that I was the only woman on his mind. I felt comforted and assured of his faithfulness by the fact that he would answer the phone at any given time that I would call. It did not matter what time of the day or night. Another indicator of his devotion to me was the way he always greeted me. Elton would not leave or come home without kissing me, and saying that he loved me. This made me confident that if a storm ever arose in our marriage, we had a love that could stand the test of time.

In spite of the difficulties within our marriage, Elton and I always found a way to function as a team outwardly. The greatest example of this came when our oldest daughter, Ashley, gave birth to our first grandchild. Our beautiful granddaughter, Milan, was born in 2010 at a time when we needed a joyful distraction. Elton was so excited about having a little one that he could watch grow up. I remember us visiting several stores to buy all the things that typical grandparents would purchase. Having Milan around hid the fraying ties of our marriage and hid our true selves for a while. Elton would always find time to spend with our grandchild. He even began to initiate short vacations at which we could include the baby. I saw this as a new dynamic in our marriage and looked forward to exploring this new chapter together. Unfortunately, the unity we found in the newness of the baby was short lived. In the hope that our grandchild would change the dynamics of our now tattered relationship, the arguments began to be more and more frequent.

One day, the Lord laid it on my heart and mind to try marriage counseling. I reasoned that the same way we tune up cars, reboot computers, and flush radiators, giving our marriage a systems check could be beneficial. When I first approached Elton with the idea, he seemed to agree. I contacted our pastor and made an appointment; however, unbeknownst to me, Elton called and cancelled the appointment. Feeling things were quickly heading down hill, I reunited with my church. I stopped trying to think of ways to repair, replenish, and rejuvenate our marriage. Instead, I was beginning to slip into a place where I was only concerned about myself spiritually. Of course, Elton was not happy with my decision. I felt that this was probably more of an attack on his pride than it was anything else.

CHAPTER 18 – SEGUE

[An uninterrupted transition from one piece of music.]

It was the most wonderful time of the year! At least, it was supposed to be. I say this because it is now Christmas time. Although Elton and I were living somewhat like roommates, we were both excited about the holiday season. My In-laws were coming to town to visit us, which meant we had the responsibility of entertaining them daily. Unfortunately, Elton did not consider this when he was making his schedule. Family time meant a great deal to me, and I thought it did to Elton as well. I planned activities for them to include spa treatments, visiting relatives, going out to eat, and many other fun excursions. In addition to the seasonal festivities of the holiday came birthday the celebrations for both of Elton's parents. Elton and I made sure that we let them know how special they were. We bought a cake and filled each night with fun and fellowship. His parents were loving people and I loved them, too. Of course, while his parents were visiting, Elton scheduled a gig. We all enjoyed the night, and Elton made sure he put on an awesome show for his parents. Right after New Year's Day, Elton's parents returned to New York. In spite of all the fun we had during their visit, I was tired. Elton told me that he really appreciated my hospitality towards his parents. I responded by saying, "You are welcome," and I hoped that this would be a turning point in our relationship. Sadly, things did not head in the direction that I had hoped.

The winter months passed, and it was business as usual. I had grown weary of disappointment, and had decided that I was going to travel and have fun -- even if it meant that I would not have my husband's accompaniment. It was now April, and I was traveling to California to attend the Price Is Right game show. Never in a million years did I expect that they would choose me as a contestant, but they did. This was truly a once in a lifetime experience. I returned home as a Price is Right winner, and Elton made sure Augusta, Georgia knew it. He arranged for a local television station to interview me; and he hosted a Price Is Right party and invited our friends over to watch me on the big screen. Elton always showed me love and affection in front of people; but I did not always see that when we were home alone. Still flying high from my Price Is Right experience and the celebration Elton hosted for me, I decided to approach my husband about my upcoming 40th birthday celebration. He told me to choose the place, any place, and not to worry about the price or the details. He told me to just charge the trip to a credit card and let him know what days he needed to take off from work.

Hawaii was our destination spot for this milestone in my life. I planned a beautiful vacation for us for four glorious days. During that time, one of my girlfriends was also vacationing in Hawaii with her husband, and when we visited the island they were on, they joined us. Elton and I made some beautiful memories on that trip. We took full advantage of the natural beauty of Hawaii, and of this special time together. It was truly a beautiful, magical paradise. I feel like my heart danced every day that we were there. Everything seemed so much more vibrant, and it seemed like the colors of the rainbow were born in Hawaii. The blues were cooler, the yellows were brighter, the oranges were warmer; and the pinks and violets were spectacular. Vacations are temporary times away from the normal routine. If I could have frozen time and kept us in Hawaii for at least a few months, I would have. However, our vacation time soon ended. No more ocean waves; no more tropical breezes; and no more rainbow colors. It seemed that when we returned home, all the love we shared was left scattered like the sands on the beautiful beaches of Hawaii.

We both had full lives – mine was filled with work and line dance; and his was filled with work and gigs. Despite this, Elton had decided to work on releasing a CD. This decision meant that he was back to spending long hours away from home – away from me. He would say that he had to spend a lot of time in the studio. I, being the trusting and supportive wife that I was, did not feel the need to question him. This type of living between us went on for months. Finally, Elton released his Gospel CD. I naively thought with the completion of the CD, we could just sit back, wait, and watch the money roll in. It was quite the opposite. The CD release came with unexpected added expenses. Elton now had to travel and promote his music if he wanted a great return. New York City was his first destination. As part of the CD promotion, he had the expense of copying the CD, making posters, purchases new equipment, and the normal costs incurred with traveling.

In spite of all of the long hours and costly operating expenses, Elton continuously strived to be in the spotlight. Local radio stations began to give him the attention that fed into the personality that he often desired from people. Not long after this newfound fame, he began to advertise his CD heavily. As a result, the checks did begin to come in and this made Elton happy. I am embarrassed now to say that I never physically laid eyes on any of the checks. At that time, I had no reason to do anything but trust Elton and he always contributed to the household financially. His passion for his music continued to develop so much so that Elton decided to write a song dedicated to me. This compilation of music included what appeared to be an outpouring of love for his family. Of course, that meant he mentioned the children, grandchild, and me in his remarks on the CD cover. His second CD release was a love CD; and I can recall Elton being on the local radio stations talking about the driving force behind this CD. I was now accustomed to him always mentioning me on the air, as well as on the stage.

I am not sure if it was BET, MTV, or YouTube spinning around in Elton's head; but he now wanted to have a video attached to one of the songs on the second CD. He did not stop there – not Elton. He wanted my line dance sisters and me to create a dance to his song, and for us to perform the dance at his big CD release party. Yes – he now wanted the same women that he had a problem with me spending time with to do something for him. I thought that he had finally changed his thinking and appreciated my friendship with my line dance sisters. I asked them and they all agreed to do it. They are a very positive group of women, and they especially wanted to support Elton in his status as a local performer, and because he was my husband. We scheduled the release party at a popular club in downtown Augusta. Elton was so excited because his ticket sales were tremendous. The night of the party was one to remember. There were so many local celebrities present; and many of my family members and friends came out to support him. One of the most memorable moments was when Elton dedicated one of the hit songs to me. If that was not enough, he blew a kiss to me from the stage. I felt on top of the world. Those who knew I was his wife smiled in support; and those who did not know who I was, looked on with envy.

Even with all of the people and all of the excitement, I kept getting an eerie feeling that I was being watched. I began to notice one woman who seemed to catch my glance all night. Throughout the entire night, it seemed that no matter where I was in the room, I would look up and lock eyes with her. I felt beautiful that night and I was both proud and happy for Elton. Maybe she liked my hair. I had cut and colored it especially for that evening. Maybe she liked my outfit. I was not sure what about me had drawn her attention, but seemed to have commanded it. Beyond the awkwardness of her piercing stares, it was a wonderful evening. Elton and I even danced to a couple of songs that night. One song, in particular, was "She's A Bad Mama Jama" by Carl Carlton. I felt like a bad *Mama Jama,* that night – *"… just as fine as I could be."* For the time being, for this one night, it felt like old times where the only thing that mattered was the two of us.

After the release party and despite the high that surrounded the CD's, Elton and I quickly returned to our normal routine. He was always gone with the band to different gigs; and as for me, I was working and going to various fellowships with my line dance sisters. In spite of the fact that romantically we seemed like two ships passing in the night, I continued to do the things that a good wife was expected to do. For example, I kept Elton's clothes cleaned, I kept the yard manicured, and I prepared home-cooked dinners daily. I felt that the rough patch we were experiencing was temporary and I vowed to do not let my appearance, my housekeeping, or my homemaking slip. I felt that since he was working hard and I was working hard, the hard work would eventually pay off to better our relationship.

One afternoon, about a week or two afterwards, I stopped at the nearby Wal-Mart superstore to purchase dinner ingredients. I was proud of the fact that I prepared hot, home-cooked meals for Elton every day. He like soul food and I know how to make all of his favorites. As I strolled around the store casually placing items in my shopping chart, a woman approached me and asked me a few general questions about hair care. I assumed she liked my hair or that she somehow knew that I was a licensed cosmetologist. Why else would someone approach me in the grocery section of the store to discuss hair care? Anyway, I answered her questions without hesitation. The woman ended our brief conversation by complimenting me on my hair. The words she spoke did not mean much at the time. In hindsight, her statement resonates with me now. Her exact words were, "Your hair **IS** always pretty." I guess my mind was on the dinner I would cook that evening because the meaning behind her statement went in and out of my ears almost instantly – it never registered. In hindsight, I now ask myself, *"Was this a happenstance occurrence? Did she just happen to be in the same store at the same time as I was? Was she stalking me?"* I am inclined to believe the latter – she had been following me.

CHAPTER 19 – MISTERIOSO AND RITARDANDO

[Misterioso: Mysterious. Ritardando: Indicates a change in tempo; slowing down.]

Our time in Hawaii remained a continuous source of fond memories – memories that highlighted my dreams on many nights. I always felt alive and rejuvenated near the ocean. Since our 10-year anniversary was coming up, I trained my thoughts to planning an anniversary vacation trip. Jamaica would be our destination. I chose Jamaica because I thought it would be symbolic to revisit the location of our honeymoon. Elton and I wondered if we would see any of the people that we met on our honeymoon, where we had all vowed to meet there again in 10 years. We were extra excited about this trip and the fact that we would be celebrating a milestone – 10 years of marriage. In fact, neither Elton nor I had been in a relationship with anybody this long, so this was truly a cause for celebration.

We set off for our anniversary trip filled with excitement and anticipation. Of course, we did not see any of the couples from our honeymoon trip, but we had a wonderful time of dining, dancing, relaxing, and creating memorable intimate moments. Jamaica is not Hawaii, but it has its own beautiful attractions. We had beautiful sunrises and sunsets; sensational sandy beaches; breathtaking views; tranquil blue seas; and we saw more people who looked like us. Jamaica has an earthy, rhythmic vibe that makes a person want to dance. The culture is modest and welcoming. The people are warm and inviting. In Jamaica, we did not feel like tourists – we felt like we were a part of the community. This was especially true for Elton. He badly craved musical success and notoriety, and he was eager to make his music known worldwide. With this thought in mind, he decided to locate local radio stations to see if they would play his music.

His finding local radio stations and getting them to play his music was not a problem for me. The problem came when he left me alone in the hotel while he did that. I had always supported Elton and his dream of stardom. I worked hard to plan this anniversary trip, and I worked countless hours on my feet to help pay for this anniversary trip. Staying alone in the hotel while he set off on an adventure was not on the travel itinerary. This could have been fun and exciting for both of us. We could have captured so many different locations and people in photos; but without a thought, Elton just left me and our anniversary plans behind while he went after what HE wanted.

Venturing out was successful for Elton. A couple of radio stations interviewed him, and they even played his music over the airwaves. When he came back to our hotel suite, he was bubbling over with excitement. I was bubbling over with annoyance and frustration when he returned. I thought it was very selfish of him to take time away from our anniversary trip to promote his CD. Elton was on top of the world and seemingly oblivious to my anger or the weight of his actions. At that point, I had a decision to make. I could continue to be upset and possible ruin the rest of the anniversary trip; or I could let go of my resentment in favor or saving the trip. I chose to take the high road, and celebrate his success. I reasoned that he took advantage of an opportunity that he might not have again (but what he actually did was take advantage of me, and my love for him). Taking advantage of me would soon become the norm with Elton. Returning home from a trip always landed us back into our familiar routine of doing things separately.

It was May 5 -- Cinco de Mayo – and I decided to visit a popular Mexican restaurant with friends. We were having a great time in an atmosphere filled with not only Mexican people, but of all ethnicities eating, drinking and enjoying themselves in unity. Unexpectedly, the woman I had seen in Wal-Mart appeared again. Of all the women there, she only seemed focused on me. She said, "Hello, Mrs. Mayweather." I returned the greeting. I did not remember ever giving her my last name and I found myself staring at her and wondering how she knew it. To divert the awkwardness, I asked her what the name of the drink in her hand was. She not only told me, but she also offered to buy me one. I politely declined, as I was not going to accept this from a complete stranger. Notwithstanding my rejection, my Wal-Mart acquaintance then asked if we could exchange telephone numbers. I gave her my number and took hers, assuming that she probably wanted to talk more about hair care. After she left the table, a few of my friends inquired about her and asked what she wanted. I responded that I did not know for sure. I told them that her name was Kendra Black, that I assumed she was someone who had seen us out and about, and that we had discussed hair care in Wal-Mart one day. We quickly dismissed the interruption and returned to our celebration.

At home later that night, I casually asked Elton if he knew Kendra Black, and he said that he did. His response made me think that perhaps Kendra had seen me at some of Elton's gigs. Again, I thought nothing of it because Elton had become quite popular as an entertainer and played his gigs nearly every weekend. She was friendly and pleasant, and gave me no reason to doubt her sincerity. *Where was my sixth sense? Where was that internal alarm that all women are supposed to have that says, WARNING – WATCH OUT – DANGER AHEAD?*

Mother's Day was upon us and Elton made sure that my day was extraordinary. Receiving cards, flowers, and gifts from my husband on holidays was a normal experience for me. On this particular Mother's Day, in addition to everything else, I received an anonymous text. The text simply said, "Happy Mother's Day." It was odd and unexpected, but I said nothing to Elton at the time because I did not want to ruin such a beautiful day. *Again, where was my internal warning system?*

When Father's Day came the following month, I showered Elton with cards, gifts, and a special dinner. I know that I went overboard, but I wanted him to know just how much I loved him and appreciated the role he accepted to be a father to my daughters. Providing a happy, healthy, and complete home for my girls had been a priority for me and I ensured that Elton knew the depths of my gratitude. Fatherhood is a huge responsibility. I was so happy that my husband loved and accepted my daughters. My happiness spilled over into everything that I did – the way I kept our home; the way I prepared our meals; and the ways I took care of him. I felt like I had it all. I had the family that I had always wanted. I had a husband. I had a home. My daughters had a loving father. I felt that I could not ask for anything more. Elton was not perfect, but neither was I. We were both works in progress. I decided to work even harder to keep our family solid. We could mend the frayed areas and firm up the areas that were already strong. We could do this. We would be just fine. I loved him and he loved me. That was all that mattered.

CHAPTER 20 – FORTISSISSIMO AND CACOPHONY

[Fortississimo: Extremely loud. Cacophony: A jarring, discordant mix of sounds that should not be played together.]

I t was now September 25, 2015. My day had been normal as it relates to working and taking care of our home. Elton happened to be off from work that day; but he had a gig in Columbia, South Carolina planned for that night. Per his routine, Elton was leaving home at 3:00 p.m., and he came into the shop to kiss me goodbye. As he was leaving, he told me that he would call me when he arrived at his destination. Like clockwork, he called about two hours later. I remember feeling relaxed in knowing that he had arrived safely.

Meanwhile, I was styling my hair because upon Elton's return from the gig, we planned to depart for New York to visit his mother who was ill. As night began to fall, there was a loud knock on the front door. My daughter, Francis, was visiting so she answered the door for me. After a brief moment, she called out to me and I noted the sound of concern in her voice. I put down the flat iron and quickly made my way to the front door.

When I arrived at the door, there stood Kendra Black. *"What is she doing here, and how on Earth does she know where I live?"* I thought to myself. Although I was concerned about her showing up at my home uninvited and I while I am sure my face most likely registered the concern I felt, I remained calm. Kendra asked could we talk. My own questions so occupied my mind that I only nodded in response. She asked if I had received her text messages, and I responded, "No". Kendra next statement was, "I know what it was like for a husband to cheat on his wife." Now, I am sure that my face fully displayed my confusion. When her words finally correlated with my understanding, I asked her directly, "Are you implying that Elton is cheating on me?" She hurriedly, and might I say happily responded, "Yes!" *(Oh hell no!)* I could not believe my ears, so for clarification, I asked her again. Her response was the same, with the same excited anticipation. Suddenly, my stomach felt queasy, as if at any moment my insides would forcibly reject the contents of my stomach. Wishfully I thought, *"Surely, this has to be a mistake. I do not know this woman and she does not know me, my husband, or anything about us."* The man that I was married to had always professed his undying love to me both privately and publicly. I did not want to allow her words or their meaning to sink into my consciousness.

I felt a toxic mixture of sadness, disbelief, pain, panic, and rage. I felt like I was an unwilling player in a Lifetime movie, like an actor in an afternoon soap opera, and possibly like the main character in an episode of Snapped. From everything I had seen in movies and on television, I knew that this situation could go from bad to dangerous in a matter of minutes. It was God's grace that stilled my heart and my emotions to allow me to stand there while this woman dumped her filthy garbage all over my front lawn. For another 20 minutes, I stoically listened and numbly nodded as Kendra dropped the bombshell that my husband was actually not in Columbia, South Carolina as he claimed to me. She disclosed that she had just left Elton in their room at local hotel, so that she could come over and talk to me.

She continued to vomit up the vile details of their regular endeavors. Apparently, this was a normal thing for them. It seemed that all of Elton's "gigs" in Columbia were actually private sexual escapades in hotels with Kendra. The longer I stood there, the more she regurgitated the nasty, sorted details of Elton's infidelity. She provided so much information, and she did not speak with so much as an ounce of remorse. Her demeanor was more that of a person who either had grown tired of waiting for the next step, or of someone who was making a desperate gesture because she feared a possible change in her status. As painful as it was to hear all of this, what was even more chilling to me was that I realized that Kendra did not only yearn for my husband; she also yearned for my life. She wanted to be who I was and where I was in Elton's life.

Adding to my disgust in the revelation of my husband's treachery, this *woman* began to describe the interior of my home. As if stabbing me with a dagger, she walked/talked me through my own home -- room by room. For the kill shot, Kendra verbally painted a panoramic image of every aspect of my bedroom décor. With relish, Kendra provided the specifics of when I redecorated the master bedroom and the new colors I had chosen for the curtains and bed linens. What kind of woman (or someone who calls herself a woman) could sleep in another woman's bed -- knowingly, willingly, and purposefully. For the same reason, I asked myself what kind of man (or someone who calls himself a husband, a father, a grandfather, a friend, a lover, a confidante, and a minister of music) could bring another woman home and commit adultery in his marriage bed. What type of cocky, cavalier, cold-hearted person could do all of this with his mother-in-law right next door? This was all too much, but somehow I was still standing.

When I did not collapse, Kendra went on to blab about conversations that she had with Elton. Based on what she said and how much she knew, it was clear that Elton had conducted deeper more intricate conversations with her than he had with me. This demon stranger, this stalker, this infidel knew all of my family's personal business. In fairness, if I call her demon, stalker and infidel, I have to ask myself to what kind of creature was I married. I do not have a background in behavioral science; but scary words I had heard like psychopath, sociopath, egomaniac, and narcissism start to swim around in my already dizzy headspace. Who was this man? How could he lie beside me night after night, profess his love for me publically and privately, and live this life of multiplicity.

To put the final nail in the coffin, Kendra professed that she had been in a relationship with my husband for 10 of the 12 years of our marriage. It was then that I felt like I was slipping into a black hole and I had nothing true to hold onto to regain my footing. I cannot explain how much I wanted this to be just a tragically bad dream; but I was wide-awake. I was standing in my front yard, and this person was standing right in front of me. After the smallest snippet of composure as possible, I looked her in the eyes and asked, "Why are you telling me this now after you have willingly participated in this deceit for 10 years." To my surprise, Kendra said, "Because now I feel like I am the other woman."

I then asked her why she would say that and how did she know. She responded, "I know for a fact that Elton has other women." To add more salt to the gaping wound in my heart, she then revealed that she had gotten pregnant by Elton. This hurt me deeply because Elton and I had a blended family, but no children together. I asked where the child was, and she replied that she had gotten an abortion.

Again, I thank God for the numbness that I felt. This type of personal attack could easily cause someone else to faint, have a stroke, have a heart attack, consider suicide, or attempt to commit murder. I did not want to believe her, but she had too many facts. The way that she doled out the information was another matter. I felt like she wanted to get an angry reaction out of me. She seemed dissatisfied when her spillage did not reward her with the response she desired. Kendra even said to me, "You are supposed to be mad." I calmly replied by saying, "No. I did not marry the women in the streets; I married Elton." Meaning, no matter what you have told me, he is my husband and I will have to wait to discuss this matter with him. At that moment, she began to cry. Much to my surprise, I felt sorry for her. What was God doing to my heart? I did not want to feel any compassion for this woman. She then moved closer to me and in her anguish, she put her head on my shoulder and continued to cry. At that point, I felt like I was living out a scene from an old cartoon – the Devil on one of my shoulders, and an Angel on the other. The Angel urged me to console her and gently pat her on her back. The Devil urged me to grab her by her hair, encircle her throat with my free hand, and choke the daylights out of her. My fight or flight instincts warned me to be cautious because she was close enough to cause me deadly physical harm. After all, she had to be crazy to come to his home with this crap. Her weeping began to escalate and I felt lost and confused as to what to do in this incredibly crazy situation. God is always on time; so when Francis interrupted us by telling me that Elton was on the phone, I was able to break our physical connection. I locked eyes with Kendra and told her that God had released her, and that she needed to remove herself from my property.

As I made my way back into the house to answer the phone, I had to grip pieces of my furniture and brace myself against the walls because my fact-riddled mind caused me to feel dizzy. Elton asked me what I was doing. I told him that I had just had a conversation with Kendra Black. He immediately responded, "I am on the way" and it seemed as though Elton made it from Columbia, South Carolina within five minutes, which would be physically impossible since it was actually 90 minutes away.

When he arrived, he wanted to talk. I just wanted him to leave. Elton insisted that we could get through this. Sadly, he tried to paint a picture that Kendra was crazy. I interrupted him by saying, "No, she is not crazy." I told him how she gave specific details about their relationship, as well as details about ours. I made sure that he knew that Kendra did not hold anything back. Moreover, when I dug into my cell

119

phone, I found the text messages that Kendra had sent and those messages confirmed even more particulars of their affair. Without another possible lie to hide behind, Elton finally told me about when and where he met Kendra. Although his details were not as precise as Kendra's were, it was painstakingly clear that I had been living a lie for 10 years.

CHAPTER 21 – LUSIGANDO, PESANTE AND DOLOROSO

[Lusigando: Coaxing. Pesante: Literally "heavy" meaning to perform the music in a manner that makes it sound heavy. Doloroso: Sorrowful.]

Elton was overly confident and his charm and charisma usually got him what he wanted; however, this situation was far from usual. I asked him to leave. Elton asked me if I could give him two weeks. The man who had lied, cheated, and made a fool of me for 10 years had the unmitigated gall to ask me to give him two weeks. The man who had just rushed over from their love nest in attempt to do damage control was asking for two weeks. The man who had repeatedly defiled our home and our marriage bed had such an inflated ego that he thought I should care about where he would now lay his head that night, or any night. Did he really think that it would be safe for him to close his eyes under my roof? Did he think that I was so nice, passive, in love or numb enough that he could just camp out at home after all of this. Either he was crazy or he must have thought that I was crazy. Still trying to maintain my sanity, my response was silent.

Elton did not appreciate that Kendra had uprooted him from his home, so he decided to return the favor. He got into his car and drove to Kendra's house to tell her husband about their 10-year affair. That is right – Kendra was married as well. My husband and someone else's wife had been maintaining a whorish relationship for more than 10 years. Not only was it dishonest and unfaithful, it was foul, nasty, selfish, and cowardly. I am not sure of what Elton thought he would accomplish, but Kendra's husband stood by her; and pretty much said that as long as things were good under his roof, he was good. I later learned that cheating and possibly swinging was a common practice that Kendra and her husband enjoyed.

Elton's anger seemed to come and go in waves. His mood changed like the weather. I felt numb and I literally checked out of any conversation with him. He talked, yelled, muttered, restated, and recanted things while I just sat there falling deeper and deeper into the black pit of despair that my husband skillfully created for me. Even though I had him dead to rights, his cockiness still made him confident that we could get past this and that I would eventually take him back. My head felt like it was about to split open, and my world was spinning out of control. Trapped inside a monstrous tornado is where I found myself. I felt that there was nothing true to hold on to anymore. There was not one aspect of my marriage that I could cling to so that the winds of devastation would not sweep me away. This tornado touched down at my home and ripped it to shreds. No foundation to stand on, no walls to lean on, and no roof to cover me. Everything was just gone!

Somewhere between reality and a murky fog, I tried to make sense of everything. I remember taking a shower after all of the devastating events of the night. I felt soiled, stained, and like Elton had completely polluted my life. I scrubbed my skin until it was raw and when I finally felt clean, I exited the shower and put on a nightgown. As I sat on my bed, it hit me. They had sex in my bed! Oh my God, I cannot sleep in here. Immediately, I began to arrange the couch so that it could be as comfortable as possible. Realizing that if I ever wanted to get a good night's sleep again, I may have to replace my bed and mattress left me bewildered. I spoke to my sister who insisted that I replace every piece of bedroom furniture. However, something in me said, "Maybe I should not." As much as I wanted to, I was quite aware that my finances were about to change; and I could not afford any more debt.

Morning appeared too quickly. I do not even remember falling asleep. It was a Saturday morning and I had scheduled my first client for 6:30 am. I tried my best to be my normal self, and I almost pulled it off. It was not until my last customer that I broke down completely. Unbelievably, my customer's daughter was selling bed sheets for a school fundraiser. One moment I was leafing through the brochure, and before I knew it, the floodgates opened and out poured my sea of emotions. I quickly excused myself to have my breakdown in the privacy of my bathroom. To my horror, I could imagine my husband and his mistress rolling around and having sex on my bed sheets. Elton could not have changed the sheets afterwards their folly, because I would have noticed and become suspicious. That meant I had lain on my sheets after they had been there. How disgusting! Who does that? I remember praying, "Dear God, help me. Help me pull myself together. Please just hold me up long enough to finish the last client." Afterwards, I thanked Him, splashed my face with cold water, and returned to my salon. I apologized to my client for my unplanned "break" and finished her hair as quickly as I possibly could.

As hurt, angry and disgusted as I was, I still had other questions for Kendra. So what did I do? I called her. I figured since she had so much to tell me before, I would just let her fill in all of the blanks that Elton would never fill. Kendra did not answer the phone when I called. However, she did return my call shortly thereafter. I told her that I wanted to verify some things that she said the night she visited my home. One of the main things that I wanted to confirm was the part about them sleeping in my bed. Of course, she did not deviate from her original story. I remember it like it was yesterday. Kendra said, "Yes Carol, we slept in your bed, but I'm sorry." I also wanted to know if she was conscious of the fact that my mother lived next door. Again, she responded with a firm yes. I thought to myself, *"What kind of woman is this? Does she have any respect for anyone?"* To me, the only way this would make sense would be if Kendra received some kind of sick gratification from being in my place and my space. What type of woman would stoop so low as to lie in another woman's bed, especially knowing that woman's mother lived right next door. I asked her directly if she wanted to be me in my house because she was so intrigued with my life and me. She did not answer my question, and our conversation ended with Kendra apologizing again for her reckless acts.

During this same period, Elton traveled up to New York to see his mom. As I had expected and true to his M.O., he was calling me religiously and apologizing for the situation. Still subject to his enormous ego, he attempted to justify his multiple-year affair by saying that Kendra gave him what I did not. I remember thinking to myself, *"What a low blow! How could he blame me for taking care of our home and taking care of him in every way possible?"* The only thing that I did not do was accompany him to every gig. I asked myself, *"How could a good wife and mother constantly be gone and have the home run efficiently?"* Turning aside from this foolishness, I began to devise a plan. The first order of business was to make sure that I was healthy. I made an appointment for a thorough examination to ensure I had not contracted any sexually transmitted diseases or infections. What a relief to find out that all was well. The next part of my plan involved securing both spiritual and legal counsel. My pastor saw me without any hesitation. His questions made me begin to put things into perspective. I also called around to check on the reputation and prices of good divorce attorneys. As I was settling in the fact that I was going to file, Elton called me from New York crying. He had just found out that the doctors had given his mom three months to live. I guess the God in me just would not let me proceed at that time. Once again, I put my needs and priorities aside out of compassion and decency. Even though I would be justified in making his life a living hell, I chose to take the high road in light of this devastating turn of events.

Elton told me that his mom wanted to see me. Of course, she wanted to see me in light of this news. We had a great relationship and she always made me feel like I was her daughter – not just Elton's wife. A week later, we traveled up there together. Even though I was empathetic and sincerely cared for his mom, I could not bring myself to tell her that Elton and I would most likely end up in divorce court. His mom had always been so nice and supportive of our union. The last thing I wanted to do was break the heart of someone I loved who was terminally ill. Although we planned to spend three days in New York with his mom, we only stayed for two days. Reason being, Elton became aggravated when his manipulation did not get him what he wanted. Upon returning to Augusta, he decided to live in a hotel until his apartment was due to be ready. Just when I thought Elton was trying to accept the divorce, he asked if we could go to counseling. I agreed to go. After all, it could not make things any worse. I also wanted to prolong time as I thought everything through.

Marriage counseling seemed like the logical thing for people in our situation to do. However, Elton forgot about one thing. He forgot that he would have to tell the truth, the whole truth, and nothing but the truth to be successful. On the second visit, the marriage counselor told Elton that he needed to put total closure to the affair between him and Kendra. As a result, Elton called Kendra that night to put an absolute end to their decade-long, sordid relationship. As a sign of "trust," Elton had me listen to the call on another telephone handset. Kendra knew Elton so well. It was obvious to me that she could tell that there was someone else was listening on the phone. For all I know, they may have already planned for such a contingency since they had been involved in this *"under [the] covers"* exercise for so many years. At first, Elton tried to play it off, exhibiting a cool, calm, collected and *never-let-them-see-you-sweat* demeanor. However, when Kendra turned the tables on him and began to speak about something that he did not want revealed, he started sweating and quickly informed her that I was listening to their conversation on the other phone. After a brief back and forth dialogue between the three of us, I asked her again, about where they had sex. I still found it hard to grasp that Elton could have managed a full-blown, 10-year affair without my knowledge – especially when it supposedly happened in my house. It was obvious to me that Kendra had flipped the script on Elton, so I thought this was the perfect opportunity to get truthful answers about where and when they met for sex. Kendra's story never changed from what she told me the day she appeared at my front door and exposed their sins to me. She reconfirmed, to the most thorough detail, that they had had sex all over my house. To add insult to injury as though that was not enough devastation, Kendra informed me that they had also engaged in sex in my daughter's house as well. More specifically, she said it was in my granddaughter's bed.

As disgusted as I was, my morbid curiosity wanted more evidence. Even though it was hurtful to hear, I had to put on my big girl bloomers and take the blows like a champion. The bottom line was, I was solidifying my divorce case and needed to give my lawyer as much detail as possible. Although it was now November, two months after the initial earthquake, I had to endure more aftershocks to gain proof. My first thought centered on the fact that my husband had used our daughter's house. Even though I had the spare key to Ashley's house, it was never her intent that we would use her home for anything. It was only for emergencies. Never in a million years would I have believed that my husband, the father figure to my girls, and *papa* to my granddaughter would have done something so terrible. Yet, Kendra's vivid recollections made it impossible to downplay any of what she said – she simply knew too much. When she described my daughter's home, it was as if I was looking at a life-sized picture. It was as if she memorized every minute detail. Kendra seemed to delight in the fact that she could accurately describe every detail of Milan's sweet and innocent little bedroom – the colors of her comforter, the stuffed animals on the bed, and the pictures on the wall. The fact that they had defiled my granddaughter's bedroom and my daughter's home was just sickening. This was straight out of a Lifetime Movie Channel movie.

Surprisingly, Elton just held the telephone handset and listened quietly as Kendra continued to regurgitate the filth that they both had practiced – or should I say perfected. Once she finished talking, she cavalierly asked if we need anything else from her. I replied by saying, "No, you have given me more than enough." I felt like I had to swallow the vomit that was starting to bubble up in the pit of my stomach. She reveled in telling me all of this, and he just sat there and listened. I was sick to my stomach, I was sick of him, and I would have to be sick in the head to stay in this marriage in longer. Having received this latest sorted and detailed information, I informed Elton that it was meaningless to see a counselor – I most definitely planned to file for divorce. Early the next morning, I began to narrow the search for an attorney. I chose one whose reviews stated that he was the best divorce attorney in town. Within two days, I was in his office and the process was so seamless that they were prepared to serve him just three days later.

CHAPTER 22 – IMPETUOSO, IRATO, AND RINFORZANDO

[Impetuoso: A directive to a musician to perform a certain passage of music in a vehement or impetuous manner. Irato: A directive to a musician to play a passage of music in an irritated, agitated manner. Rinforzando: Reinforced; emphasized; suddenly, abruptly reaching a height.]

I felt as if my life was reeling out of control. I was having a physical and emotional breakdown. Even with the majority of Elton's personal things gone from my home, I just could not stop the thoughts that ravaged my mind and sense of inner peace. My home was supposed to be my refuge -- the place where I felt safe and secure. My husband was supposed to be my protector -- the person to stand guard over my home and my heart, and not allow anyone or anything to hurt me. Instead, my home became their love nest and my husband was a co-conspirator in the attempted demise of my emotional wellness. Moving about in my home became a daily struggle.

From time to time, my friends would often pick me up and take me out to lunch or dinner, just to get me out of the house. I usually entered my home from the carport, through my sunroom, and then through my salon to the kitchen. One day, after having lunch with a friend, she dropped me off in front of my house, and I entered at the front door. The first thing that I notice upon my entrance was Elton's piano. He did not take it when he moved his things out of the house. I cannot remember whether he did not have space for it at his new place, or if he left it behind so that Milan could use it for piano lessons. Whatever the reason, it now stuck out like a sore thumb. Every time I looked at it, I thought of him. I could envision him sitting on the bench, playing it and singing. I did not want or need any reminders of Elton in my home. The same way that Elton had to get out of my house, his piano had to go, too!

I became obsessed with getting rid of this piano. Everywhere I went, I would ask if anyone wanted a piano. I made announcements at church, at dance class, and in my salon – "Piano – free to go home. If you can pick it up and carry it away, it is yours." I was not interested in selling it. I did not want one red cent for it. I just wanted it gone. It was just a musical instrument; but I felt like I had deep-seeded hatred for it. That piano was what Elton used to practice and create his music, write his songs, and dream of his stardom. One of his songs, "Sensual Woman", used to be a source of motivation for me. At his request, my line dance sisters and I created a line dance to this song and we performed it at two or more events for him. I remember feeling so special because I thought that I was the "sensual woman" he was singing about. Now, I realized that it could have been Kendra, or a myriad of other band groupies with whom Elton was acquainted. I did not need or want any more reminders of Elton in my home. The piano had to go. Not only did I remember and imagine him sitting there and playing it; but it also stirred up bad comparisons for me.

Elton played me, just as he played that piano. The piano was always right there waiting for his attention, just as I was. There were many days when he hardly noticed the piano, which was just how he treated me. When he spent time playing the piano in the early years of our marriage, beautiful music filled our home. Likewise, when Elton *seemed* interested in nurturing our relationship, we made beautiful music together and our home life was happy. Now, years had passed since he even bothered getting the piano tuned. He had long since stopped tickling any ivories in our marriage, since he apparently had other keyboards across town. Now, it was a dusty, out-of-tune, forgotten piece of furniture; and that is pretty much how I felt. I doubted if any aspect of our relationship was every truthful. Elton was a master gamesman. He played with my feelings. He played with my health. He played with my mind. He played house with someone else in my house. The bottom line is that Elton played a dangerous and unforgivable game with my life. This big, dark, bulky thing seemed to laugh at me every time I walked past it. Actually, I felt that many people were laughing at me. Many people felt sorry for me. Many people knew what was going on long before I did.

Unfortunately, every time I thought I had someone lined up to come and get the piano, that person would back out. There were so many let downs. I wanted that piano gone, but I did not intend to spend any of my money trying to get rid of it. I had enough debt associated with my life with Elton, and I was determined not to spend another dime in that regard. That piano was a big, brown, dusty, and out-of-tune, tangible reminder of 12 wasted years, and I sincerely wanted it out of my house. There were times when I detested the presence of it so much that I imagined myself dragging it out of the front door, off the porch, down the sidewalk and out to the driveway. There, I would have doused it with gasoline and had my own bonfire in true "Waiting to Exhale" style.

I had plans for my home. I wanted to redo the house in its entirety. Getting rid of the piano was a priority; however, I would not allow it to become a roadblock to prevent me from moving forward with the planned overhaul. Yes, I said OVERHAUL. I was determined to remove every single trace of Elton from my home. This man defiled my home to the lowest possible degree, and I had to erase it all in order for it to feel like home again for me. I felt like I was fighting for my sanity and emotional wellbeing. I purchased this home before I met Elton. This was my property and although he did not physically take it from me, he succeeded in taking away the feeling of refuge, serenity, and safety I used to feel when I crossed my threshold. I had to make this MY home again, and the only way to do that was to rip out every inch of floor he ever walked on, every door he opened, and every doorknob he ever touched. I did not know when, and I did not know how; but I had faith that God would make a way out of no way.

CHAPTER 23 – TRANSPOSITION

[Playing the music in a different key.]

Elton's mother passed away in November. It was Elton's best friend who called to give me the news. He went on to tell me how distraught Elton was and how much he needed me. Either Elton had not shared the condition of our marriage with his friend, or he was using his friend to get me to have pity on him. Knowing Elton, I believe both cases were true – his friend did not know, and Elton was using him to try to soften my resolve. There was nothing too low for Elton. He even tried to use his mother's death to manipulate the situation in his favor. Not falling for it, I provided Elton's best friend with a brief synopsis of

Elton's 10-year whore *"capade."* I told him that I would have to pray about contacting Elton at all. I did just that. I prayed and asked God to lead me to do what He would have me to do. After much prayer and analyzing the situation, I called Elton. All I could think about was the fact that Elton had no one, and that I did not want to do anything to block my own blessings. The Bible teaches forgiveness and reminds us not to harden our hearts. Elton had lost his brother, his wife, and now his mother. I contacted him and expressed my sympathy. Elton accepted my condolences; and then went on to apologize and repeatedly say that we could work on our marriage. Understandably, it was not the time to talk about our marriage and I would not allow him to sway me from the purpose of my call. Therefore, I quickly turned the conversation back to the subject of his mother, and I stayed on the phone to be a stoic shoulder while Elton vented his grief. I ended the conversation by asking Elton to inform me of the funeral arrangements.

In view of the sad circumstances, Elton took advantage of this period of bereavement by calling me every day. As par for the course, Elton thought only of himself, and about what he wanted. It was almost as if he had a convenient case of amnesia when it came to all of his dirt – or perhaps he thought that there was a problem with my memory. There was no way that I could forget a hurt that deep and a betrayal that long. I fully comprehend the term *"love is blind."* When I was deep in the throes of loving Elton, I was blind to his selfishness, ego and conceit. Now, it was as if those defining characteristics were flashing from his person like neon lights. I remember feeling embarrassed knowing that all my family and friends had long before recognized the *"all about me"* traits in Elton that recently became visible to me. Regardless of what I felt for him personally, I booked a round-trip flight to New York to pay my final respects to his mother. When I told my family and close friends about my pending trip, they could not believe that I even considered going. I explained my reasons and they eventually came around. My mother had two concerns -- my emotional wellbeing and she did not want me to miss our traditional Thanksgiving dinner. However, she respected my final decision and my efforts to do the "right" thing. My dear sweet mother arranged to host our traditional Thanksgiving dinner a few days early, so that we could dine together as a family.

On the flight to New York, my mind tormented me with thoughts -- some of them were good, while others were very bad. Once I arrived in New York, the tormenting did not desist. I tried my best to concentrate on the funeral for Elton's mom, but I could not help but think of all that I was going through. Once I arrived in New York, Elton picked me up from the airport. I could tell that he wanted things to be as normal as possible. For example, he greeted me with a kiss as though nothing had ever happened. I did not want to make the trip any more unbearable, and I did not want to invite inquiring minds into my business, so I complied with the charades. Our destination beyond the airport was to go directly to his parent's home. After I greeted everyone, I jumped into action and began to cook and clean, and do whatever else I could to be helpful. It was better for me to keep busy in that space, and I was determined not to bog down Elton's family with our marital problems.

The home-going service for Elton's mother was very nice. I was so glad that I attended. After the funeral, Elton and I had moments where we could talk. I took advantage of this time by informing him that I was definitely divorcing him. He responded by saying that, "we didn't have to do that." I also told him it would have to be God's will to restore our marriage; otherwise, it just would not happen *(it would have to be God because I was not going to lift one finger to work on this mess)*. He did not like my response, and as he did in times before, Elton became angry and ultimately shut down. I concluded the conversation by telling him that I had already filed for divorce, and that he could expect to receive the declaration soon. The morning after, I headed for the airport to travel back to Augusta. Even after everything that he had done to me, it still stung to realize that this would probably be my last time in New York City as Elton's wife. As the car passed all of the famous landmarks and places we had visited, my mood quickly changed from okay, to melancholy, and to sad.

Daily life back at home in Augusta now included gathering many documents for the attorney. The divorce process was moving very fast. It is funny how one can be married for several years and be able to dissolve the marriage in a matter of a few quick months. I wondered what was going on with Elton now that he knew what was coming. In any event, I did not have to wonder long. Elton called me the day he received the divorce papers. He coquettishly asked how all of this worked. He went on to say that because he had been the plaintiff in his other divorces, he did not know what he was supposed to do as the defendant/respondent. I did not fall for his poor acting, and just listened to him go on with his monologue. At the end of the conversation, Elton expressed that this was too much for his understanding, and that he would secure an attorney, as well.

The New Year came in with much uncertainty for me. I had just endured the holidays without my husband. Although, my family and friends were there for me, there was still somewhat of a void in my life. I assumed that Elton was going through something as well because he reached out to me by way of sending flowers. The flowers were beautiful and they smelled very nice; however, flowers just could not save the day anymore. Flowers did not make the pain go away. Flowers could not erase the years of his illicit affair. Flowers could not rid my memory of hearing someone tell me to my face that she had christened every room of my home by sexing my husband. Elton could have sent every flower from the Tournament of Roses Parade, and it still would not have been enough. The realization is that Elton had dumped a truckload of sh*#t on my doorstep, and he could never have enough shovels to dig his way out or to remove the stench of his filthy behavior.

It was now January 4, and here I was in divorce court. Quite naturally, I was nervous. I did not know what to expect. As I entered the courtroom, Elton made his way towards me. Without any greeting or cordialities, he simply handed me an insurance document that I needed. Soon after we sat down, court began. The judge went over the specifics of the case. In addition, both lawyers presented their cases. In the end, the judge ordered that the divorce would be final in three months. I did not want my face to reveal the relief that I was feeling; but I am sure that some of it showed. In spite of everything discussed, the judge still viewed all of the text messages between Elton and Kendra. He saw and heard the evidence of the hell I lived because of their dishonesty and infidelity. My attorney had warned me that the outcome of divorce cases were unpredictable. In the end, I received a pleasant surprise. Reason being, I had asked for alimony to help me get back on my feet from all of the marital debt. My attorney stated that he was not sure what the outcome would be. Not only was it favorable, but also it was more than we had asked for. As I sat and heard the outcome, all I could do was thank God.

One would have thought that this was the end, but Elton's lawyer had more tactics in store. A few days later, he requested my bank statements and other documents pertaining to the house. I am to presume that Elton's attorney was trying to say that I was lying about my income. Likewise, Elton ended up having to disclose his financial documents. Despite the attempts to reduce the alimony as well as belittle me in court, the judgment still stood.

I will admit that Elton and I had dinner a few times after I filed for divorce. I will also admit that I still had lingering feelings for him. I genuinely loved Elton for all of the years of our marriage. The feelings in my heart were in serious battle with the good sense in my head. Part of me wanted to be absolutely and without a doubt certain that it was over; part of me wanted to know if he possessed any redeeming qualities; and part me wondered if, at the very least, we could somehow be friends. I was not just thinking about me. Part of my motivation for being friendly with him was for the sake of my granddaughter, Milan. Her "papa" was her world; and I did not want to be the one to cause her little world to come crashing down. Nonetheless, the goal of our friendship was unattainable. I can now say that it was for the best. I can recall it like it happened yesterday.

One night while we were on the phone, we ventured into a conversation that took us back to the affair. After a brief dialogue, Elton informed me that he was still seeing Kendra. Translation: They were still cheating; they were still lying; and they were still dishonorable people. At that very moment, I knew that divorce and a total eradication of all ties to Elton was necessary. I could no longer attempt to be even his friend. When a person genuinely feels remorse about something, that person would move away from that thing – discontinue that hurtful behavior. Elton had not changed. He was a slave to his ego and his lust. He had mastered the arts of deceit and betrayal and believed that he was like Teflon – no matter how hot the pan got, nothing stuck to him. Elton did not have any respect for me, for Kendra's husband, or for Kendra for that matter. I honestly do not know how either of them were able to face their own reflections in a mirror on a daily basis. This man was not worthy of my friendship, my conversation, or my time. I also reasoned that if he thought so little of Milan that he would take his mistress to her home and have sex in her bed, he was not suited to be her "papa" either. Elton had wounded me to my core, and I knew that it was only through God's grace and mercy, that I was still emotionally whole. I simply could not and would not allow for Milan's exposure to any future hurt by him. Once closed, some doors should remain closed! As far as I was concerned, any door leading to Elton was certainly a door to slam closed, lock, board up, and barricade. Through the grace and strength of God, that is when I bowed out gracefully, and ceased all communication with Elton.

Soon spring had sprung! I wanted to use gardening as my therapy. At least once a week, I would go out into the yard and work, meditate, and pray. I often wondered if I ever knew what love was. I wandered if there was there something in me that I needed to change. I often asked God what He had in store for me. Questions and more questions would often sneak up into my mind. Although time was passing quickly, the answers to my questions were not coming quickly. I soon realized that if I allowed myself to reflect on my life and tried to make sense of everything, I did not accomplish much gardening; therefore, I would clear my head and focus on the feeling my hands in the soil. I knew that in the end, the soil would bring forth something beautiful and alive.

Instead of allowing my mind to become idle and giving Satan a playground to destroy me, I decided to focus my time and attention to family. In spite of all that was going on, I still had some joyous days in my life. Elders would often say that after each death, God blesses a family with new life. My marriage and relationship with Elton died, but shortly afterward, God blessed our family with the birth of my first grandson. Francis gave birth to a beautiful baby boy, Connor. This was the first baby boy in the family and we were all immediately smitten with him. Instead of pinks and lace, we shopped for cute little outfits in robin's egg blues, mint greens, and sunny yellows. No more ribbons, bows and headbands. In their places were one-piece rompers and the cutest little caps. We bought baby jogging suits, blue jeans, and tiny little Nike sneakers. God's timing was perfect then and remains perfect today. He knew just what we needed and when. What a heartwarming and timely event for all of us.

Still keeping with my forward stride, I planned to join my friends on a cruise to celebrate my godson's graduation. At first, I was excited about getting away. I only envisioned looking out onto the water, relaxing, meditating, and having a good time. I did not really hone in on the date of the cruise when I planned it; but I later realized that the departure date was my wedding anniversary. My pending divorce, the storm that I thought I could weather, soon turned into a tropical hurricane. Just like the hard rains of hurricane season, an endless surge of tears born in my heart poured from my eyes.

My best friend felt so sad for me that she offered to alter some of her plans. As much as my misery needed some company, I insisted that she not ruin the vacation for herself and her family. When the ship docked for land excursions, I opted to stay on the ship so that my godchildren would not see me do nothing but cry. I took that time alone to really rest and think about my new life. Although I was glad to be getting the divorce, there was still a deep sadness within me for what could have been. The four days and three nights of the trip seemed like an eternity; but I made the best of it.

After the cruise ended, I decided not to directly return to Augusta. Instead, I spent time with a cousin in Florida. It was refreshing to see her. We dined at popular eateries and laughed about old times. I chose not to venture too much into discussions of my plight in life. The negative energy had already robbed me of too much happiness. I could not change what I could not control, and I prayed daily for God to grant me serenity and acceptance. Vacation was over, and my new reality awaited me at home. Returning to Augusta would be different from all other times. Instead of coming back home to a husband, I would be returning to an empty nest. It was all over. There was no one there to cook for, clean for, shop for, primp for, or long for. It was just me, myself and I. I knew, deep down, that divorce was the best possible resolution – after all, Elton never truly committed himself to me. I will never know if he ever intended to, or if he even knew how. My sense of logic needed a place to place the blame firmly. I knew that my marriage ended in failure; still I tormented myself daily wondering if I could only blame Elton for failing me, or if I had somehow failed him.

After dealing with those thoughts for a few days, I realized that I needed to do something constructive; so I decided on construction. I remembered how much I hated the fact that my home had been so vilely defiled. I decided to use the alimony money to renovate my home – and my mind at the same time. I hired a building contractor who designed a new, and more open layout for my home. I had him tear off every door, every doorknob, and all the floors. He knocked out walls and tore down cabinets. I needed something good to come from that relationship and something tangible that I could see every day.

In the midst of all of this construction, the piano was still in taking up space in my living room. On any given day, there were strong, able-bodied men working in my house and I could have gotten the contractor or his workers to take it off my hands. However, I decided to keep it after all. Instead of it being a reminder of Elton and his dirt, it could now be a reminder of what and how God brought me through. Instead of feeling shame, regret, or imagining that this thing *laughed* at me, I could now smile victoriously when I walked past it. God restored my peace. I decided that I would polish the piano and make it a centerpiece in my living room upon the completion of the renovations. It would forever symbolize how God gave me a new song to sing.

CHAPTER 24 – FIN AND OMAGGIO (THE FINAL NOTE)

[Fin: End. Omaggio: Homage, celebration.]

Weeks and months passed, and finally something besides the weight of my divorce had taken a front seat in my thoughts. The renovations to my home were well underway and I was growing impatient with excitement waiting for the finished product. My house was literally a construction site, and with so many areas simultaneously under construction, I spent most of my time on the back corridor traversing from the salon, to the computer room, then to my bedroom, and vice versa. I must admit that I am a proud and very organized "neat freak," and dust and clutter make me crazy. In this case, however, I knew this was something I had to go *through* in order to get to the other side – the better ending. Still it took all of my will power not to follow behind the workers with a damp rag, broom, dustpan and mop all day. To pull my focus away from the dust and clutter, I would often find a quiet place either in my salon, the computer room, or my bedroom to read.

I had been browsing, off and on, through one particular book in my salon during breaks between my clients and sometimes at night before bed. I recall that at the onset of my season of turmoil, a customer gave me that book to read. The book was a sort of self-help guide for other women who were experiencing difficulty. Although I had only ingested a few chapters, this book greatly motivated me. I was nowhere near finishing the book, but the fact that the author was brave enough to put her experiences on paper really affected me. Suddenly, I realized that I had not gone through all of this just for me. As I reflected back on my entire life, I realized that I had a story to tell, and in that moment, I decided to write a book. I endured many trials and tests, and God brought me THROUGH to the other side. This would not be tell-all book for some reader's curious gratification; rather, it would be a book for every reader's positive edification. It would be my testimony. It would be a true account of how love and commitment can exist against all odds. It would show other womn that when that when necessary, God could and would provide the strength to strike the final note; and then give you a new song to sing. Sharing my narrative would be a flight propelling me into a newness of self-worth, victory and triumph!

Oh yes, I can say that striking that final note was of God, because His word tells us when divorce is permissible. God created me in His likeness and for the purpose of praising and magnifying Him – not anyone else. It was not His intent that I be a doormat for Elton or anyone else to walk over or wipe their feet on. I had spent far too many years supporting Elton's dreams, praising Elton's accomplishments, and magnifying Elton's *celebrity*. In return, I received lies, betrayal, deceit, humiliation, and even debt. I realize now that even before marrying Elton, my priorities where not in the proper order. I was trying to create the perfect family, but I did not realize that without God as the foundation, anything that I tried to build would eventually crumble and fall. I endured so much, and I can only give the credit to God for holding me together and bringing me through the fire, through the storm, and through the hell I endured on Earth. God is not a respecter of persons; therefore, what He did for me, He can and will do for anyone else who trusts and believes in Him. If God is for me, who can be against me? Likewise, if God is for you, who can be against you?

Some may think that this was a lot to go through to get to this point; but I now know that all of this was necessary. I had to learn to lean to God's understanding and not my own. I had to learn to wait for His timing, and not my own. For so many years, I had attempted to mold, shape, and create a family unit with my priorities out of order. My focus had always been outward – thinking of everyone and everything else first. This journey allowed me to do something that I had never done before. That is to focus totally on me. I had to learn that I am worthy of love, respect, and commitment. His word tells me that I am fearfully and wonderfully made. Now, for the first time in my life, I had to look in the mirror and make some life adjustments.

The first thing I wanted to do was complete my high school diploma. My sister, Angel, suggested that it would be a good time to focus my energy on something positive. I was always embarrassed whenever I disclosed that I had never completed high school. People always assumed that I had completed high school because I was a homeowner and business owner for so long. I knew that education was very important. I had even instilled this core belief into my children. Now that my children were adults, I could make my education a priority. Admittedly, I feared jumping back into school pool with both feet. It had been so long since I attended school, and I did not want to drown. I knew that I could do it, but I needed to build up my confidence. Taking all of this into consideration, I started out very slowly. Once I realized that I could do it, I began to schedule consistent study times, and even worked with tutors. Managing demanding work and study schedules was extremely challenging; however, I knew that I could do it and that I had to do it for myself. Never in a million years, did I think that writing this book would be nestled into my plans; but I know that God intends for the tests that I have endured to become a testimony that I may share with the world for His glory.

As I stated earlier, I wanted this book to be a valuable teaching tool to all who read it. I wanted to share the lessons I learned about **faith, trust, love, forgiveness,** and **waiting** while on the journey to overcoming.

- *"**Faith** is the assured expectation of what is hoped for, the evident demonstration of realities that are not seen." (Hebrews 11:1)* We cannot buy faith; no one can sell us faith; and as much as we would like, we cannot give or get faith to or from someone else. Without faith, we have no place with God, and we definitely cannot please Him.

- *Trust is an assured reliance on the character, ability, strength, or truth of someone or something.* Trusting someone means that you THINK that person is reliable, you have confidence in him or her, and you feel safe with him or her physically and emotionally. There is a significant difference between trusting humankind and trusting God. God is not a man and he cannot lie. I think it is important to do all things as unto God, and trust Him to take care of us.

- *Love as defined in the Bible is the union of a man and a woman who make a covenant before God to fulfill their God-given duties to each other in marriage. The Bible instructs husbands to love their wives, just as Christ loved the church. The two are to become one flesh.* In today's world, marital love has taken on slightly different compositions; however, the concept of one committed, solid union remains the same. The Bible also teaches that we must love everyone – yes, EVERYONE – if Heaven is our goal. This was a huge river for me to cross. As you can imagine, it is very easy to justify your anger, resentment, and even hatred when you are the injured party. I accept that I must love everyone and rid my heart of ill will; however, that does not mean that I have to love everyone up close and personal. It does not mean that I have to invite everyone into my home or my circle. I chose to let the love of Christ live in my heart and guide my steps. I learned that I can and have to love some people from a healthy distance.

- ***Forgiveness*** *is critical for a healthy relationship with ourselves and with others.* The Bible states that when someone hurts us, we MUST forgive that person. It is a mandate from God. If we cannot forgive, we cannot expect forgiveness from God. It is an acting of pardoning an offender. We forgive others when we release the resentment and do not seek payback for the hurt or loss that we have suffered. It does not mean that we forget, it just means that we release the burden of holding on to that enormous weight in our hearts. As women, we tend to share our plights and situations with others seeking empathy, sympathy, or just company for our misery. After doing so, we sometimes allow the peer pressure from our friends and family to dictate what we do and how we do it. Unsolicited advice comes from all different directions and in listening that advice, we base our actions on our quest not to "look stupid" or like a "wimp".

- I have learned that forgiveness is more for the forgiver than the forgiven. Letting go of the hurt and the pain made me calmer, improved my health, and increased my happiness. It is important to remember that a person should not seek new love if carrying the baggage of old hurts.

- ***Waiting.*** Such a simple word, but one of the hardest tasks. The Bible teaches that God acts on our behalf as we wait for Him. *"But those who wait on the Lord will find new strength. They will fly high on wings as eagles. They will run and not grow weary. They will walk and not faint." (Isaiah 40:31) "Yet the Lord longs to be gracious to you; He rises to show you compassion. For the Lord is a God of justice.*

Blessed are all who wait for Him." (Isaiah 30:18). When going through a difficult season, it is important to remember is to wait *EXPECTANTLY* to see how God will answer. Think of the eagle while reminding yourself that an eagle flies to a high spot and wait for the storm winds to come. When the storm hits, it sets its wings so that the wind will pick it up and lift it above the storm. While the storm rages below, the eagle is soaring above it. The eagle does not escape the storm; it simply uses the storm to lift it higher. Therefore, when the storms of life come upon us, we can rise above them by setting our minds and our belief toward God. The storms do not have to overcome us; we can allow God's power to lift us above them.

We may never understand all the mysteries of God's master plan. We may never understand why He allows us to experience trials and hardships. However, our Bible tells us that ALL things work together for good for them that love God. Oh yes, I love Him. There were moments when I have questioned my every decision as I have stepped into this new life. Regardless of those thoughts, there was always an inward cheerleader telling me that I could make it. My life has not been easy, but it has been full of rewards. These rewards included me understanding that I had not lost everything, to include a hope of marital love. Sometimes life may throw us many curve balls; but nothing is more rewarding than standing on your faith knowing that in the end Got promises restoration and VICTORY.

This is definitely not the end ....

This is the start of a

NEW beginning,

and the best is yet to come.